The Oracle

Books by Edwin O'Connor

THE LAST HURRAH
(*Atlantic* Prize Novel, 1955)

BENJY

THE EDGE OF SADNESS

THE ORACLE

The Oracle

by EDWIN O'CONNOR

An Atlantic Monthly Press Book

LITTLE, BROWN AND COMPANY

BOSTON · TORONTO

ATLANTIC—LITTLE, BROWN BOOKS
ARE PUBLISHED BY
LITTLE, BROWN AND COMPANY
IN ASSOCIATION WITH
THE ATLANTIC MONTHLY PRESS

Published simultaneously in Canada
by Little, Brown & Company (Canada) Limited

PRINTED IN THE UNITED STATES OF AMERICA

To my mother and my father

The Oracle

one

IT WAS LATE SEPTEMBER, AND THE SUMMER HAD NOT YET gone. All day, the normally temperate city had sweltered, and now, as darkness approached, the heat remained: a sullen, humid blanket of air, so unfairly blown north from subtropic muck. . . .

In the broadcasting studio, the temperature was scarcely endurable; the air conditioning had failed unaccountably more than two hours before, and had not been repaired. Christopher Usher, attempting to beat the heat, had removed his clothing; for the first time in his career he was naked as he broadcast to the nation. Squares of cardboard had been hastily placed across the studio windows, shielding him from the gaze of the curious or the prurient. White and pink and intermittently hairy, he sat poised before the microphone, and as he read from the pages of his script, little globes of sweat bubbled, burst, and raced down the meaty concourse of his trunk. He was uncomfortable, but he was not unhappy, for he was *talking*: it was the scheduled hour of his nightly communication with his public. As he read from the script before him, he addressed the microphone with an air of personal persuasion, as if it were an agreeably unenlightened companion, as if, under the ripe sigh of his baritone, it had become magically endowed with the property of conscious audition.

". . . higher taxes for everyone? Uncle Sam to say to you and to me: 'Now just hold still while I cut myself another slice of that family dollar; don't move, this won't hurt a bit!' Well, a lot of big men in Washington are saying that it's got to come. They're saying that when more money goes out, more has to come in. They're saying: 'That's just good old-fashioned arithmetic, and we ought to know, we're economists!' Well, ladies and gentlemen, I'm no economist, but like millions of other Americans, I *do* drive an automobile. And I know that when that automobile starts going too fast, starts getting out of control, the good old-fashioned remedy is *not* to give it more gas, but to start thinking about putting on the brakes. . . ."

He read on, moving and bobbing with the words, lending each phrase gymnastic emphasis. Christopher was a big man, a solid man, and at the age of forty-five, he was in excellent physical condition. A slight tendency to fat he controlled by exercising vigorously each morning, clad in a curious all-rubber garment which was styled like a child's pajamas. From time to time he fasted, following a diet of his own devising. He was not a particularly good-looking man: his face was large and rather granitic, the type of face often seen in group photographs of professional football teams. It was redeemed from any suggestion of brutality, however, by the eyes: they were large, pale-blue, and rather pious. As of the past few months, they were also mildly presbyopic, and as a result Christopher was forced to hold his script at a distance which was not altogether comfortable. There was the alternative of wearing glasses, but although Christopher prided himself upon being without personal vanity, he found in this suggestion something singularly distasteful.

Leaving national affairs for the moment, he turned to Europe. He had little time for Europe tonight; he contented himself with recommending a plan for the furtherance of Western European unity. . . .

". . . adoption of English as a common language by France, Italy, the Benelux countries. The language of Chaucer, the language of just plain John Smith, so admirably suited to the breaking-down of ancient barriers of mistrust and fear! Think it over, you gentlemen who have the fate of a continent in your hands. This is not the time for false national pride. . . ."

Whenever possible, he preferred the simple solution; here was the common sense out for the inheritors of Dante and Racine.

He left Europe and moved far to the East, to China, and here he paused to expand. He liked China; he knew China; he had even been there. He had seen this land under conditions of peril when, as a correspondent during World War II, he had journeyed there barely a year after the cessation of hostilities. He had remained there for four, almost five weeks; he had seen Chungking, the Bund, the Great Wall, and Chiang Kai-shek (twice). He had been deeply moved by the little yellow men, scurrying so docilely through filthy streets; in their enigmatic faces he had discerned a peasant contentment, of a kind unknown to people who ate regularly. He had been impressed, even flattered, by the elaborate courtesies extended the distinguished visitor; not here, in this subtle cocoon of hospitality, was to be found the occidental brush-off. He had grown thoughtful; he had seen that there was something here worth preserving; he had left China a friend. It was a friendship which did not wither under the adversities of battle. . . .

". . . China hopelessly lost? Beaten into the dust by the boots of Mao Tse-tung and his Muscovite masters? Well, not according to this observer. I say we can't sell the Chinese short. I say that the sob-sisters who cry 'Give up! No more money down the rat hole!' don't know China, don't understand China. I say they're badly under-estimating the Chinese little man, the coolie; under-estimating his loyalty, his pride, his willingness to fight for the things he loves. This afternoon I talked for two hours with a man whom the late, beloved Vinegar Joe Stilwell called one of the most remarkable military minds in Asia. He had hope, courage, assurance. 'Give us the guns, the planes, the money,' he said, 'and leave the rest to us. . . .' "

Perspiration gushed; broad bare buttocks twitched in rebellion on the unpleasant perch of wet leather. Christopher talked on, unheeding; in the happy moment of autohypnosis, he was immune to physical misery. Because China was so important, he gave it forty-five seconds more; then, wrapping it up, he came back home for a driving finish with the heartening domestic items from which his broadcasts derived their special flavor. He talked of a Day for Grandparents, of a newly discovered miracle an-algesic. He talked of schooldays, with a nostalgic footnote on the early days of his own educational experience. He talked of a happy Hollywood marriage; of a new method of sucking cheap heat from the earth; he talked of a hero cat. . . .

". . . what inscrutable Providence watches over children and the pets they love. Tonight we know that little Rose-mary Chaplin, of Decatur, Illinois, is reunited with her kitten, Amber . . . that same kitten whose love and alertness saved the life of its little mistress . . . fire broke out in child's room . . . kitten's frantic mewings roused dormant household . . . fire extinguished, but Amber overcome . . . death feared imminent . . . Rosemary's prayers . . . stroke of fortune . . . famous veterinarian visiting in city . . . rushed to scene . . . skilled fingers on furry body . . . touch and go . . . at last . . . heart-warming conclusion to a story of loyalty, fidelity, *faith.* . . . "

He continued, his pace accelerated by emotion, the rich pump of his voice flooding the living rooms of the land with knowledge, hope, inspiration. Like all members of his authoritative profession, Christopher dealt harshly with the world and its people when they failed, as they so often did, to meet the standards that he had established for them. However, he differed from many of his colleagues in his refusal to become discouraged. He was an optimist. His primary task, as he saw it, was the communication of this optimism, as a kind of tonic, to his fellow citizens. To this end, he forever probed the dark clouds of human endeavor for the barely discernible ray of sunshine. When he talked daily to the great and the near-great of ruin and disaster, he never failed to pluck from these conversations some wisp of cheer. Above all else, he was the apostle of the pneumatic sidelight. In a world where budgets soared and taxes swelled, where nations muttered in mutual infelicity, where the footfalls of the dispossessed echoed hollowly through the night, Christopher uncovered the deeds of possible redemption:

a dictator dancing with his aged mother at a state ball; a United States senator manfully hurling his sagging frame through a Kiwanis romp; a Boy Scout bandaging a puppy's paw. These were the human, the homely cores, the silver linings around which Christopher could expand in moving, often memorable fashion. He was not an unsentimental man, and sometimes, as he read the words which he had written, he was touched; occasionally he wept.

He had been broadcasting in this manner for close to nine years. He was popular with his listeners; he was extremely well paid. . . .

After the broadcast, in the little bathroom off his office, he took a shower: it was a slow, voluptuous procedure, suds as thick as whipped cream melting in the warm, nozzled rain. Outside it had grown cooler; a sudden shift of wind had brought the smell of the sea across the city, possibly signaling the end of the heat. He smiled and hummed in satisfaction; as he dried himself, he thought of a new derisive nickname for the President.

As for the broadcast, he reflected that it had been one of his best. He was pleased by this, but unexcited; excitement was for the beginner. For Christopher, long accustomed to the production of the distinctive, there was merely a pastoral euphoria, an awareness of public responsibility, expertly discharged.

He dressed quickly, for he was to join his wife at a dinner party across the city. Friends were giving it: companionable people, eager to learn. He reached for his hat, and prepared to leave, then paused to jot down a memorandum. On the following evening he planned to devote a portion of his broadcast to an analysis of Soviet public opinion; for the sake of certainty, he would contact authority.

Phone Louis Budenz, he wrote. Then he went off to the party.

"Christopher, you are the *soul* of my party," said Mrs. Edwina Branch, swallowing a final shred of lettuce, and placing the empty plate upon the sideboard. She was a large woman who moved like a confident man. "I'm so glad you could come!"

"I'm afraid I can't stay very long. I have an appointment down town."

"Wait," she said, moving off. "At least wait until I've brought you some of your devoted fans. They've been *dying* to meet you!"

Waving admonishingly, she disappeared in the crowd; Christopher, wrapped in disappointment, watched her go. He had been let down badly, for the dinner had proved to be a buffet. It was a style of dining which had always annoyed him, lending itself as it did to fragmentation. He stood in the center of Edwina Branch's dining room, awkwardly balancing a plate of cold turkey and potato salad, gazing at all the people who had fled into independent, buzzing groups. It was not from such that conversation grew, that an audience was formed, and he longed for the cohesive force of the central dining table, with everyone fixed immovably in assigned position. At the moment, under this system of regrettable mobility, he was left with no one, not even his wife. . . . It was then that he saw her hurrying to him across the room.

"Christopher. Did you just get here?"

"Yes." Bobbing his lips toward her cheek in a sweep of perfunctory passion, he inquired after her well-being by asking: "Were you able to hear the broadcast?"

"Yes, in the library, dear. I got here just a moment before you went on. Very good tonight, I thought."

"Not bad," Christopher said, "considering everything." He spoke in the objective tone with which he was accustomed to weigh his own achievements, and went on to describe, in some detail, the broadcast to which his wife had so recently finished listening. Slender, blond, with a cool, small, agreeable face, she stood, smiling slightly, head tilted to one side, occasionally inserting a brief, punctuative murmur. Now in her early forties, Meredith had been married to Christopher for twenty-one years; to her marriage she had brought intelligence, patience, and the amount of humor necessary for survival. It was this last which sometimes troubled Christopher. He knew that somewhere, deep within this woman who was his wife, lay a small, alien spring of irreverence, a spring that at the most inconvenient moments—when he was establishing a point, say—would spurt without warning, and a bright and mocking bubble would dance across the path of calm attention. Although this did not occur too often, it was nevertheless a disquieting potential, and it was because of it that Christopher determined not to mention to his wife that he had broadcast in the nude that night. There was nothing *funny* about that fact; he knew that, but still, he knew from experience that it was precisely the sort of thing that sparked the secret smile. . . .

"Well," he said, concluding, "so much for the world at large. Anything new at home?"

"No, not a great deal. Another package of decayed fruit arrived this morning. Isn't there some way you can stop it, Christopher?"

"I don't see how." Some weeks before, on one of his broadcasts, Christopher had come out strong for fresh fruit. He had spoken glowingly of boyhood days upon the farm, of firm-fleshed apples, of sweetly succulent pears; he had spoken with resignation of the sorry substitutes available to him in the city today. The response from rusticity had been overwhelming. A torrent of home-grown produce poured in from impoverished orchards; crates and boxes of warty, stunted fruit, in varying stages of putrescence, had been delivered to the Usher door. There had even been a case of vile-smelling preserves which had leaked a glue-like, irremovable syrup over everything. Christopher found it all quite touching.

"They're good people, Meredith," he said. "If the fruit is bad, we'll put it in the compost pile. Were there any telephone calls?"

"Only two. The dog hospital called: a Dr. Duquesne."

"Yes, he's the director. What did he want?"

"Just to thank you for your check, and for your broadcast about the hospital. He said it was deeply moving; apparently some of the nurses cried."

" 'Puppies Go to Surgery'? Do you know, I've had more mail on that than on anything I've done in months? It's still coming in. Naumetz wired that Hollywood may use it as the basis of a documentary. What was the other call?"

"From Mrs. Rogers, late this afternoon."

"Mrs. Cedric Rogers?"

"Yes."

He swore briefly. "It's not hard to tell what *she* wanted: another free talk. What's the occasion this time?"

"Well, she was rather vague, but it seems that the Republican Mothers are getting behind the Eye Bank. Your presence at the fund-raising meeting would be appreciated. She didn't mention anything about a fee."

"No, you bet she didn't. . . ."

"You don't suppose she wants you to give an eye?"

He glanced at her suspiciously. "It's no joking matter. Every time a few dollars have to be raised for some cause, it's Christopher Usher to the speaker's platform, gratis. God knows I've always done my share and more for charity, but there's a limit!"

"You always *could* refuse, you know."

He shook his head. "Not with Cedric Rogers' wife in the picture; it's the same old public-spirited blackmail.

No, I'll do it, but they won't get anything special. I'll give them 'Gandhi and Christ' and they can like it or lump it."

Although Christopher was far too self-sufficient to believe in God, he firmly believed in the efficacy of the religious process for those less fortunate. Accordingly, he spoke of Him frequently on his broadcasts, and he had prepared a number of platform talks with what he called "the spiritual twist." "Gandhi and Christ" was the least imposing of these. He had written it some years ago, in a hurry; it had been intended for filler material, to be used whenever the time or the recompense did not allow the "A" treatment. A brisk study in comparative sanctity, it wore well; Christopher had delivered it for years now without change, save for the necessary alteration in tenses following Gandhi's death. Undoubtedly, he thought, it was the ideal stuff for the Republican Mothers.

"By the way," he said, suddenly remembering, "I'm going to have to leave early tonight. Senator Marble's in town, staying at the Ritz just for the night; I want to catch him before he goes back to Washington. You won't mind going home alone, will you?"

"No, certainly not. As a matter of fact, Father's looking in before the evening's over, and I'll get him to take me. But it's a shame you have to go back down town again tonight. You wouldn't like me to drive you?"

"No, no." He reached out and patted her hand. "You stay here and take care of Edwina," he said, "and leave the United States Senate to me."

"Poor, poor Christopher. All work and no play . . ."

Christopher smiled ruefully. "The penalty of fame," he said, half-humorously. He looked around the room, and something of his former gloom returned. "This is a very poor party," he said querulously. "All spread out like this; I'm surprised at Edwina."

"Christopher, shhh . . ."

For Mrs. Branch came striding toward them, a rather singular-looking couple in tow.

"Prepare, Christopher," she sang, "to meet two of your most *ardent* admirers! Kilgallens, this is Christopher: a guiding light in a darkened world! Meredith you've already met."

"My greatest booster," Christopher said, smiling gently at the supporting words.

"It was Christopher and Christopher alone who kept me going throughout the war," said Mrs. Branch, nodding rapidly. "A *tower* of strength! Christopher, tell us all about the world; the Kilgallens have been *dying* to hear it from your own lips!"

Mrs. Kilgallen, tall and toothy, uttered a cascade of honeysuckle laughter. "Indeed we hay-uv, Mistuh Ushuh," she agreed, the southern voice dripping musically from the long, angular body. "Ah'm jus' *mad* abaht yoah towks. The count and I wun't *dream* of missin' one!"

"The count?"

The man beside Mrs. Kilgallen coughed. "I'm a papal count," he said. He was an excessively short man, with

13

sandy hair and a head like a tough red vegetable. "Fact is, Mr. Usher, my wife and myself have been listening to your broadcasts for years. They're good. Quite good. She listens every night, I listen whenever the pressure of business allows. I've heard most of your talks on China. I liked them." He coughed again. "Fact is, I'm quite familiar with China myself. My business brings me many Chinese contacts. Close contacts. I know—"

Christopher shifted his feet and said swiftly, "Ah yes, China." He recognized the presence of a competitive spirit. "It's a strange and tragic land, and offers a difficult problem," he said, slipping easily into gear. "Difficult, but by no means hopeless. It's largely a question, as I see it, of the will to resist, of the Chinese people themselves. That's what we in the West must understand. By that I mean that the problem of China is not similar to that, say, of Czechoslovakia."

"China's a vast country," said Count Kilgallen, nodding knowledgeably. "Can't lose sight of the tremendous amount of territory involved—"

"And while the factor of land, of sheer physical space, is of some importance, the big difference is on another plane entirely. It's in leadership. The Czechs, for example, had none. You'll say Beneš," he said, putting up a hand, for the count appeared dangerously close to opening his mouth, "but although I knew Beneš and liked him, I realized that at the end of the war he was a broken man: broken in body, broken in spirit. . . ."

"Betrayed by those he trusted," said the count hurriedly. "Fact is, however, China—"

"And that," said Christopher, "left only Masaryk. A small man in a large role, woefully miscast by history." He spoke as if he were quoting, which indeed he was. "Jan Masaryk was weak; weak and sly. I never liked him, and from my observation the Czech people came around to share that point of view. But China's pattern of leadership is something else again. China is not without a guiding force, a strong man. China still has Chiang. . . ."

"The li'l 'Gissimo!" cried Mrs. Kilgallen, clapping her hands. "He's one o' the count's very fay-vrit people, in't he, Count?"

The count coughed and said: "Remarkable man. Fact is—"

"A remarkable man indeed. I think," said Christopher slowly, "that beyond doubt, he's one of the most remarkable men it's ever been my privilege to meet and know."

"You know him!" exclaimed Mrs. Kilgallen. "Count, Mistuh Ushuh knows the li'l 'Gissimo!"

"Yes," said the count shortly.

"Temme, Mistuh Ushuh, when you wuh towkin' to the 'Gissimo, did you get the feelin' he was awful . . . shoat?"

"Shoat?"

"She means short, poor dear," said Mrs. Branch, with a burst of hearty baritone laughter. "Darling, you southern belles! Christopher, I don't know why on earth it is, but

15

Sally has this fixation of the *heights* of men!" She cast a meaningful and not entirely surreptitious glance at the diminutive Count Kilgallen.

"Good many of the world's great figures," said the count with some truculence, "were not exceptionally tall men. Napoleon, Dollfuss, Mussolini, Stalin . . ."

It was along such frivolous bypaths that the heart of wisdom drained away; Christopher resolved to plug both leak and count simultaneously.

"Of course it has no direct relevance to the Chinese problem as a whole," he said, gently reprimanding, "but I should say that judged by the standards of his own people, Chiang would be considered quite tall."

"Awmmmm," said Mrs. Kilgallen, in a vast, sub-Mason-Dixon sigh. Mrs. Branch uttered a brassy titter, and the count's little vegetable face took on the color of a deep bruise. With no small satisfaction, Christopher continued.

"The important thing, the thing we can't afford to forget, is the personality of the man. The force that makes the man what he is. What we have to understand is that he and those about him offer the one hope to a resurgent China . . . a promise for the future . . . a promise to which a humble, war-weary people can look with hope, with confidence. . . ."

Without further interruption, he developed this theme at some length; under his benign analysis, the Kuomintang gradually took shape as an organization not basically dissimilar to the Boy Scouts of America. It was only a chance glance at his watch which brought him to an abrupt, summative sentence; like most of his instructive talks, this one had an interior flexibility which permitted it to be pinched off at any point without the slightest effect upon its meaning. Indicating the necessity for his departure, he made hurried amenities, and, with Meredith, effected a quick retreat. Mrs. Kilgallen followed him with large, violet, vacant eyes.

"In't he wown-duh-ful, Count?" she breathed.

The papal count was not altogether of the same mind.

"Gabby bastard," he said.

At the door, Meredith said: "You won't be too late?"

"No, but don't wait up for me, in any event." He bobbed her another kiss. "I'll be as early as the law and Senator Marble allow," he said, rather jauntily. His recent triumph had placed him in the best of moods. "Give my best to your father."

Leaving, he met his father-in-law on the front steps.

"Ah, Doctor," he said cordially, in spite of the fact that, although he respected his father-in-law, he did not entirely like him. Dr. Edmund Wrenn was an aged, immaculate little wraith of a man, with faded blue eyes, and an excessive urbanity of manner which Christopher sometimes suspected. "How are you this evening, Doctor?" he asked.

Dr. Wrenn greeted Christopher in his customary fashion by wincing slightly and proferring a cold, chalky paw. "You are your usual, vigorous self, I see," he murmured. "*Mens sana in corpore sano.*"

"I try to keep fit. Of course I'm not as young as I used to be."

"So few people are," said the doctor. "Well now, tell me, how is the world of sport these days? Baseball, for example? The 'pennant races,' I believe you call them—are they proceeding to your satisfaction? Are you 'rooting home' the local team?"

An expression of strain crossed Christopher's face. Like many of his colleagues in the business of global omniscience, he had prepared for his vocation by serving for a number of years as a sports columnist on a metropolitan daily newspaper. Released from this crucible nine years ago, he now, although by no means ashamed of the experience, rarely referred to it. Dr. Wrenn, on the other hand, referred to very little else.

"I'm afraid I haven't had too much time for baseball this year, Doctor," he said stiffly.

"No? Well, no doubt you have your reasons. Possibly you have been too busy looking ahead to the arrival of 'King Football.' I cannot blame you in the least; when I was a very young man, I found it most exciting. The hollow 'plunk' as toe met pigskin in the annual gridiron classic between the Sons of Eli and the Men of old Nassau. It stirs the blood, eh, Christopher?"

"Yes. Good night, Doctor."

"Good night, good night."

Inside the house Meredith kissed her father and said: "I wish you wouldn't do that."

"Do what, my dear? My, my, you look very pretty tonight; very like your poor mother."

"You were teasing him again; I heard you. You know perfectly well that he doesn't do sports any more."

"My dear, do not attempt to bait an old man. Of course your husband does sports. That is his *raison d'être*: he is one of our most conspicuous authorities on all sorts of running and jumping around. What else would the man possibly talk about?"

Meredith smiled; a loyal wife, she nevertheless could not manage to be suitably indignant with her father. "All right," she said, "I'll stop if you will."

"Now that sounds fair," said the doctor, sitting down. "Tell me," he said, "what *does* your husband talk about these days? Which corner of the world currently merits his attention? Germany Infelix? The Italian Riddle? Or could it be Sly Bruin to the North? Which one, I wonder? I so rarely listen to the radio."

"China. Chiang Kai-shek, the Kuomintang, et cetera."

"The Kuomintang, no less! Dear me!" A look of exaggerated distress swept across the old face. "He has abandoned Europe? As I remember it, the last time I listened to him—which was a very long time ago, incidentally—he was speaking in a positively intimate fashion of such things as the *Reichswehr*, the *Front Populaire*, and *Fasci di Combattimento*. He was really quite stern with them. I remem-

19

ber thinking to myself at the time that it represented something of an advance for a man accustomed to scolding professional wrestlers."

"Father. . . ."

"And now he has shifted his sights once more. Or is it simply that he *outgrows* continents, as little boys do their clothing? I wonder?"

Meredith sighed. "This is all so pointless. I do wish you'd make an effort to like Christopher, Father. He's really extremely nice. . . ."

"I find this exaggerated loyalty preposterous," said the old man. "You resemble your poor mother in many ways, my dear: she was quite capable of forming these violent, unreasoning attachments for the most improbable people. Although," he qualified, "there is at least this to be said for your mother: she did not go so far as to marry one of them."

"The trouble is, of course, that you just won't give him a chance, even after all these years. I admit he *does* talk a lot, and sometimes he *is* a bit pompous, but you might at least recognize some of his good qualities. . . ."

"Why is it," the doctor asked pleadingly, "that we can never discuss your husband without these excursions into fantasy- *Good qualities!*"

"He's very generous, kind—"

The old man groaned. "Stop, stop! You have already gone too far!"

"—and you'll have to admit that he's done well. From

20

that awful little newspaper job he had when we were married, right up through the ranks to where he is now. . . ."

" 'Right up through the ranks,' " echoed the old man in distaste. "You are beginning to believe in this fiction yourself. I admit nothing. Your husband is an opportunist, a creature of circumstance. He has two simple and rather unenviable attributes: a remarkable talent for the commonplace, and that ridiculous lachrymal voice which appears to be standard equipment for describing to great numbers of idiots the catastrophes they are currently enduring. As we live in an age of catastrophe, as well as of idiots, it is not surprising that your husband has done well. The fact that he is of limited intelligence is not a drawback; to the contrary, it is a decided asset. He brings to every problem in statecraft the uncomplicated instincts of the sports reporter. All the world is a playing field: the international *coup d'état* becomes the rough equivalent of the quarterback sneak. . . ."

"And of course," said Meredith, with some finality, "there remains just the possibility that I am rather fond of him, and he of me."

"And that, of course," said her father courteously, "is where I am defeated. Let us talk of something else."

And father and daughter talked on into the night; not of Christopher, but of other times, other places, other people: a long, affectionate journey through the golden past in which memory peeled away the years, and Dr.

21

Wrenn became once more young, erect, unwrinkled, confronting a pale-blonde, motherless little girl in the nursery. . . .

Christopher drove to the center of the city; he did not stop at the Ritz. Instead, he continued north for several blocks, finally parking in front of a large, aggressively modern building. He locked the car, looked around quickly, and hurried into the small, chi-chi lobby.

"Ah, good evening, Mr. Sinclair," the desk clerk said, suddenly appearing: a plump, glossy, epicene young man.

"Good evening." Christopher hurried along; he preferred to enter and leave the building unobserved. Still, as the elevator doors closed behind him, he could not help but congratulate himself upon the shielding alias. Walter Sinclair. . . .

In the lobby, a lone bellhop jerked a thumb toward the elevator. "Who?" he asked, for he was new on the job.

"That, my dear, was Christopher Usher," said the desk clerk. "The news commentator. The naughty man is friendly with Miss Andriescu in 1405."

"Woo woo," said the bellhop, rolling wise adolescent eyes.

"Animal!" said the desk clerk, flinging him a roguish glance. "Such *instincts*. . . ."

On the fourteenth floor, Christopher stopped at a door and let himself in with a key.

"Lura," he called, looking around the sitting room. It

was a setting provided by a management sensitive to the taste and requirements of its clientele: the dazzling, zigzag striping of zebra wallpaper melting into the orchid ceiling set the tone of the room. Everything here was familiar to Christopher: the great plastic fireplace with the imitation glowing coals; the polar bear rug, woven of purest spun nylon, and invitingly juxtaposed to the heatless fire; the tasteful nude paintings, originals all, done by de Berber of Los Angeles; an ivory-tinted television set, and over it an ivory cross that glowed purple in the dark; the inevitable box of bonbons, already half-devoured; the voluptuous divan on whose hairy zebrine cushions certain exciting depressions indicated the recent presence of a recumbent body; above all, the heady delicious scent of Lura everywhere. It was only Lura herself who was missing, and Christopher called again.

"Chris baby," said Lura, coming into the room through a side door. Lura Fontayne Wisper Andriescu (born Etta Pendergast) was a woman of pneumatic luxuriance: flowing blue-black hair, a ripe, dark-cherry mouth, curved, at the moment, in an expression of mystery; dark glossy eyes that glowed invitation beneath elaborate penciled arches; and a full and mobile body that seemed about to wriggle out of its sleek sheath of dark satin.

"I was in the john," she apologized throatily.

Christopher winced, and she hastily amended the error; she sometimes forgot that the direct speech of West Coast courtship was not agreeable to him.

23

"I mean the little girls' room," she said delicately. "Did I keep my lover-man waiting a long, long time?"

The lover-man smiled strongly. "I could wait for you," he said (a trifle awkwardly, for he was as yet unskilled in the locutions of flirtation), "a very long time."

"Mmmm, *nice*. Such a pretty thing to say. After that, I'd be a rude, rude girl to keep my lover-man waiting. And I *mustn't* be rude, must I?"

"No," said Christopher, moving toward her. "No, Lura, you mustn't be rude."

Later, these coy preliminaries and their somewhat hectic consequences completed, the two lay side by side and Christopher said: "I'll tell you something, Lura. Do you know how I did my broadcast tonight?"

"Mmmm, no. . . ."

"In the nude."

"You mean *raw-raw*?"

"Stark naked," he said, with quiet pride.

A scented, playful hand tapped his cheek in mock reprimand. "Chris *baby!*" she said. With the deep, primitive wisdom of her profession, Lura understood the superfluity of words; in moments of crisis, she expressed herself by pantherine twists and variously modulated sighs. "Chris *baby!*" she said again, the inflection indicating appreciation of the bold and naughty deed.

Christopher smiled and then said, teasingly: "I was thinking about you today."

"Mmmm, I *hope* so. . . ."

24

"I was thinking you might be getting tired of us here in the East. I was wondering if, all of a sudden, you might not decide to pack up and go back to Hollywood. . . ."

"*Hollywood!*" The word was a moan, and Lura's facile eyebrows dipped in pain. "Not Hollywood, please, Chris baby!"

It was for Hollywood that Lura had abandoned her native Indianapolis, ten years before: an eager young woman with high hopes and an unrivaled figure that wiggled when she walked. It had been a discouraging experience. Bit parts in three small-budget pictures, a pair of disastrous marriages, and an endless round of indecent proposals: it was fun, yes, but was it *progress?* A little sadly, Lura concluded that it was not; the only remedy, she thought, lay in escape, a silent withdrawal to some remote corner where her wounds might heal, her fortunes increase. And so she had come East, slipping away from the film capital in a silence so complete as to be slightly disconcerting.

"No, not Hollywood. Never again."

"Good." He gave her a protective little squeeze. "That's the kind of talk I like to hear."

"Oh Chris baby, I couldn't go back. It's so *artificial* out there. Everything and everybody is so . . . so *artificial.* . . ."

Christopher nodded in understanding. "An unhealthy world," he said, "of make-believe."

"Yes, that's what I wanted to say. And what have they got?" she asked, stirred to a rare, passionate verbosity by

25

the remembrance of past indignities. "Nothing but oranges and Jews . . ."

"Now, now!" Instinctively, he looked around uneasily, for he had recently been appointed an honorary chairman of the League of Interracial Friendship. "Anti-Semitism is wrong, Lura," he said. "Dead wrong."

"But Chris baby, who's anti-Semitic? I even married one. Bubu Andriescu's father," she said, with a touch of pride, "was a very famous Rumanian Jewish prince. But Bubu was cruel; you'd never believe the things he tried to do to me! And then to run away to Rumania after the divorce. . . ."

Christopher said gravely: "You mustn't judge an entire people, Lura, by the actions of one scoundrel."

"Mmmm, you're so tolerant, Chris baby. Such a *big* man," she murmured, indignation swiftly dissipated by the exhausting effort at dialectic. "You're *real*, Chris, not artificial. There aren't any Christopher Ushers in Hollywood."

He waved a disclaiming hand.

"No, I *mean* it. That's one of the things I love about you, you're so *wrapped up* in your work. And I'm so interested. Tell me more about it, Chris baby. Tell me," she said, "more about Japan."

"Japan?"

"Yes. The other night, remember, you were telling me all about Japan. I *loved* it."

"As I remember it," Christopher said, somewhat

26

coldly, "I told you a few things about China. I don't remember ever having mentioned *Japan*."

"Did I say Japan? I *meant* China; you know how bad I am at geography, Chris baby. Tell me everything about it."

And so Christopher talked about China. It was this blending of the physical with the catechetic that made their relationship so thoroughly satisfying to him. He sometimes thought that he liked best of all these moments when, the first excitements over, the warm, healthy, marvelously vital creature beside him, after a series of brief, snuggling movements, grew quiet, and passively awaited the molding of the virgin putty of her mind. It was slow work, for her powers of retention were not great, but she was flattering in her willingness to learn, and Christopher had no small confidence in his own instructive powers.

He talked on for some time and finally Lura twisted lazily and murmured: "*China.* What a wonderful, wonderful country. I always thought that someday I'd like to live there, Chris baby. I was in a picture once about China; I had to wear *sapphires.* . . ."

"Sapphires? Why?"

"I was the White Ranee who was captured by this Chinese bandit prince. Every night he used to make me put on sapphires and dance for him. Of course I had to give them back to the studio every day, but you should have seen them on me. The make-up man said my flesh was just right for sapphires. Would you think I had good flesh for sapphires?"

"Yes, yes. . . ."

"When I had to give them back for good," Lura said, "I cried a little. . . ."

After a pause, Christopher said slowly: "How would you like to have a nice little sapphire all your own? One that you'd never have to give back to anyone?"

"Oh, Chris baby, no! I didn't mean it *that* way. . . ."

"It's entirely possible that one of these nights I may come in with a surprise for you. A surprise that glitters!"

"But you shouldn't! You've given me so many wonderful things already you make me feel like a wicked woman!" She supported the rebuke with a particularly viscous kiss. "I'm so expensive to you," she sighed. "This lovely place, all these beautiful, *beautiful* things. . . ."

She fell silent, thinking again, as she did so often, of the miracle of her meeting with Christopher, seven months before. It had been at a cocktail party to which she had not been invited, but to which she had gone anyway; *that* had been no problem. She had been near desperation: her financial reserve, always perilously low, had now disappeared, and the volatile Bubu Andriescu, upon whom she depended for precious alimony, had long since fled the country, and now rested in some Carpathian fastness, secure from the bailiff's arm. She had owned only what she wore on her back, and not all of that; she had been searching for someone, anyone—and she had met Christopher. Within her limitations, Lura was a swift and accomplished workman; that very night Christopher had begun his first prolonged gesture of marital infidelity.

"No," she said. "You're too good to me. Everything costs so much. . . ."

"Don't you worry about that," Christopher said. "I want you to be happy, Lura. Besides, I'll tell you a secret: in a few weeks, I'll have a rather large increase in income."

"More money?" said Lura, not unalertly. "Chris baby, how wonderful for you! But how?"

"My contract renewal talks come up very soon now. I'm submitting a new set of demands. You'll be part of my increased cost-of-living plans. Will you like that?"

"Mmmm. You're so smart, I think you could do anything, I honestly do. But I worry about being so expensive to you. . . ."

"I'm not complaining," he said. He looked at her and gave her a playful pinch; it was time for the things of the mind to take a back seat. "I'm not complaining at all," he said.

"Oh, Chris baby. . . ."

Much later, Christopher came home to find the house in darkness; Meredith had gone to bed. He let himself in quietly, tiptoed to his room, undressed quickly, got into bed, and went to sleep immediately. It had been a long, rewarding, and not untypical day.

two

CHRISTOPHER'S BROADCASTS DID NOT EVOLVE WITH THE easeful magic of clouds in the summer sky. Before they were spoken, they had to be written, and although the writing itself presented no problem (on the sports page Christopher had acquired facility of expression; now, writing in the graver idiom of humanity, he had achieved the peak of his productive powers, and as one after another the plump, heartening phrases spilled from him, he realized that he was writing better than he had ever written before: with dignity, wisdom, beauty, speed), behind the writing lay a daily program of research and

reflection almost Carthusian in its inflexibility. It began
in his office each afternoon at two o'clock.

First of all, he read his mail. He did not, could not,
read all of it: out of the huge, ever-renewing flood his
secretary, a polite, efficient young man, sieved a score or
so of the more representative letters. These were brought
into Christopher, and he read them with pleasure. In the
main, they were highly approving, but Christopher considered even the sour notes: a turbulent blast of Old
Testament epithet from a prominent labor official; several
challenges to public debate from Unitarian clergymen; a
letter from Norman Thomas. He read these, smiled, and
threw them in the wastebasket. Then he passed on to
more congenial reading:

Dear Sir:

Your stirring broadcast of Friday last, in which you so ably scored
the taxation policies of the current "administration" merits the
appreciation of every right-thinking citizen. It is high time that
a man of courage called attention to the criminal waste and
negligence which are fast driving this once great country into
the role of a second-class power. Your views coincide exactly
with my own; I wish to God there were ten thousand more like
you!

If you should be in Seattle in the near future, please feel free
to call upon me. I should deem it a pleasure and a privilege to
see that every facility of our splendid city is made available to
you. . . .

Appreciation from civic authority came often; it was
always welcome. Christopher placed it aside for filing,
and moved on:

Dear Mr. Usher:

It gives me great pleasure to inform you that at the last semi-monthly meeting of the Improved Order of Red Men, Oak Park Chapter, you were selected as the outstanding radio commentator of the year by unanimous vote.

We wonder if by any chance we might present this award to you in person? Each year our chapter holds its annual dinner-dance on the third Friday in December, at which time it is our policy to present some figure of national importance to address us. In view of the above mentioned vote, we would be delighted if this year you could be that speaker.

Would you kindly write us and let us know whether you would be able to attend? And also, if a fee would be expected? While we have a small budget set aside for such purposes, we are not a large chapter. . . .

During the year, Christopher went off on several lecture tours; in addition to providing revenue, they enabled him, as he said, to "keep in touch." On the margin of the letter he penciled brief notations to his secretary: *Thank for honor; check mid-December schedule; if can do, Gandhi & Christ, $200, EXPENSES.* He was his own lecture bureau, and he had discovered, long ago, that a modest fee, plus expenses, could prove far more lucrative than a flat, all-inclusive fee of a much larger size. He went on to the next letter:

My dear Sir:

For reasons too obvious to mention, I sign this preliminary letter to you with a pseudonym. My real name? It would mean nothing to you, therefore. . . .

I will come right down to things. During the last year of the war and also until recently I was in the government employ working for the development of atomic power. A big cog? No, but always in the position to see what did go on.

For more than a year and a half, side by side, I worked with a man who today is a power in the atom program. I distrusted him always, why I do not know. I observed him on all occasions, and because of my learning in those days it is by no means astonishing to me that a certain land across the sea has now the secret of the bomb.

Everything I say to you I can prove. Many, many national magazines suspect I have this story and press me about it. But because I listen to you on the radio with great admiration I would prefer you to be the one to bring my story to the American people. If as a sincere patriot your interest is aroused you may contact me by . . .

Unimpressed, he pushed it away. In general, he was content to leave the fertile field of the exposé to a more aggressive colleague, a man whose envenomed bite had been felt by most of the responsible public servants of his time. As for Christopher, it was not normally his cup of tea. It was, at best, uncertain work, demanding long hours, untiring investigation, and the final untidy contact with the Un-American Activities Committee. Still, he was not a prude: there were times when he enjoyed a good, lively, confidential betrayal, and in a way he rather regretted that this was not one. Unquestionably, it was spurious; worse, it was not exclusive. It was a carbon copy, and he wondered idly how many of his colleagues had received identical offers that day. He passed along to the next letter:

Dear Mister Usher,

Thank you thank you and God bless you for all the good things which you say on the radio every night to which I and my dear husband Becker listen. There is not a night goes by I do not get down on my knees and Becker does too to pray for you and ask The Good God to let you keep on with your good work for many many years. . . .

Of all the letters he received each day, it was response of this kind which pleased him most. It constituted by far the greater part of his mail, arriving in plain, smudged envelopes, upon which had been superimposed improbable postmarks. This one came from a small community in Arkansas; he noted this without surprise, for he was exceptionally strong in the Bible Belt. Vox populi, he thought comfortably; in the homely, semiliterate outpourings, it was possible to detect the heartbeat of a nation. This, he knew, was his real public: this lovable, untutored, but infinitely educable core. Toward it he felt a sense of dedication verging upon the mystical. It was not, fortunately, a unilateral affection; reciprocity came in the form of letters of faith and appreciation, as well as in the vast purchases of the nasal unguent which had sponsored Christopher's broadcasts from the beginning. He thought with fondness of this immense and loyal band, and as he thought his lips automatically formed usable little phrases: a living natural resource of this our ample land; diamonds in the rough whose rich gleam warms a nation. . . .

At home, Meredith read a telegram with distressed eyes. It read: DEPART LOS ANGELES TUESDAY 0900 PLANE UNEXPECTED ASSIGNMENT IN EAST POSSIBLY CAN STAY

WITH YOU DAY OR SO LOOKING FORWARD POWWOW
BLACKBURN.

Telegrams of a similar nature had arrived, at irregular
intervals, ever since Christopher had become acquainted
with General Walter Blackburn, shortly before the out-
break of war. They were now fast friends; no one—and
certainly not the general's military superiors—regarded
this elderly warrior more highly than did Christopher.
That the friendship had ripened to such an extent was
due, in large measure, to the nature of the general's
duties during the war.

For some reason consonant with the national security,
the general had not been given an active command.
Still, he had had his function; it had been an innocent
and nomadic one. From the moment of Pearl Harbor
he had been ordered out on the road, speaking at rallies,
selling War Bonds, building morale in remote and in-
accessible corners of the land. For the duration he had
continued to follow the tiring, eccentric itinerary which
had been designed for the specific purpose of keeping
him physically removed from Washington at all times.
He had been vaguely resentful, he had even grumbled a
bit, but like a good soldier born and bred he had done
his duty, and it was in the performance of such that he
had come to be Christopher's military confidant. Often,
en route to his far-flung objectives, he had stopped at
the Ushers' home for a spell—Meredith, remembering,
could see the fierce, erect old figure, resplendent in olive-

greens, striding up the front walk, followed by an enlisted man staggering under the weight of the rich, ox-
blood luggage—and there, before a crackling fire, a glass
of port in his hand, he had talked with affection of the
glorious days of World War I, and with regret of the
young men of small promise who, by unfathomed
stratagem, had been pushed far beyond their natural
capacities: Bradley, Marshall, Eisenhower. . . .

The memory of each such visitation now returned to
Meredith with a startling clarity of detail, aiding her
appreciation of the promise of "powwow" contained in
the telegram. She had no difficulty in envisioning long
hours of high-echelon conversation, as the special revela-
tions of the two men would combine agreeably and
ceaselessly, filling the library with clouds of words which
would stretch far into the first dark hours of the
morning. . . .

"Damn!" she said. "Oh, damn, damn, damn!"

She knew that Christopher, when she told him the
news that night at the theater, would be genuinely delighted.

In his office, Christopher had finished the reading of
his mail, and now began the actual preparation of his
broadcast. The world had bubbled while he had slept;
his desk was piled high with records of the overnight
doings of the human race. There were neat piles of tele-
typed dispatches from the wire services: AP, UP, INS,

Reuters. There were the daily newspapers; each day he read the *Times*, the *Herald Tribune*, the *Journal-American*, and the *Christian Science Monitor*; it was thus he attained balance, proportion. There were the country weeklies which had arrived; although less timely than the dailies (with the exception of the *Monitor*), they served to provide a sturdy, indispensable, rustic pulse. There was his private news letter, a lengthy and somewhat ponderous roundup of fact and hypothesis mailed to him nightly from the national capital by a venerable ex-senator turned tipster.

In addition, there were the magazines: *Life*, *The National Geographic*, *Quick*, *Time*, *Newsweek*, *Asia*, *Popular Science*, *The Infantry Journal*. These were the periodicals he had selected as being more or less essential to his professional survival; disparate in character, each contributed its special essence to the rich stock from which Christopher drew so freely. They were supplemented by a number of lesser-known journals which, although valuable, were, because of their sectarian nature, restricted in scope: *Red Cross Facts*, *Hygeia*, *The American Indian*, and *Pal*. The last-named was an antivivisectionist quarterly; it was sumptuously produced, and edited with appeal and imagination. On the front cover was a photograph of a partially dismembered collie; under the picture ran the legend: "VIVISECTION IS AN UNMANLY CRIME!"

Beyond the newspapers and magazines, there were also books—a permanent reservoir of analysis and conclusion which Christopher seldom consulted. Years ago, in that transient moment of uncertainty (and even some self-doubt) which had followed his departure from the sports page, he had hastily acquired several volumes which, he hoped, might support him in the preliminary hours of his new calling. For almost a month he had plowed through the heterogeneous classics: Clausewitz, de Tocqueville, Marx, Spengler, Major George Fielding Eliot. It had been arduous going, and not too rewarding. Then, suddenly and beautifully, he had realized that it was all nonsense, that the problem was not one of growth, but of simple adaptation, that the Old Christopher with the Old Equipment —faith, compassion, understanding, style—was more than adequate to this larger arena. The uncorrupted Usher Point of View, transferred to the macrocosm—*that* was the answer. He had stopped all reading immediately, and from that moment he had done well. His library remained on the office shelves, a dusty, humbling memento of shameful days of self-mistrust.

He began to examine the newspapers, his practiced eye roving quickly up and down the columns in search of truth, corroboration; the two, in his experience, were seldom mutually exclusive. He marked with a red pencil those items which would be first assimilated, then converted into the ripe undulance of broadcast diction. In addition to the routine items, he concentrated on the food and clothing advertisements, for he had decided that it was high time for another body blow at the high cost of living. He delivered these frequently and effectively, employing the simple economics of nostalgia: a pork chop, a quart of milk, the two-trouser suit; how cheap at the turn of the century, how dear today! To reinforce his position, he told the vivid story of offal: animal innards, rejected as dog food or mulch in the abundant days of our ancestors, now gracing American tables at a dollar a pound. He scribbled rough notes: he condemned the human consumption of entrails; he recommended a buyers' strike, a temporary shift to vegetarianism; he drew the happy picture of frightened meatmen, their freezers bursting with unsold roasts, falling to their knees in supplication. He turned from sweetbreads to Italian land reforms; then to a border dispute in Pakistan; and then his work was interrupted by the entrance of Mr. Churchill Chan.

The two men talked, generally, of China; particularly, of China in relation to Christopher.

". . . express gratification on behalf of my unhappy land," said Mr. Chan, with a fluid little bow. He was an ageless, graceful Cantonese, a vigilant sentinel of the Kuomintang. "You are striking mighty blows," he said. "One could not ask for more."

Christopher shifted in his chair, his forehead wrinkling in deep thought. "I wonder about that," he said. "As a matter of fact, I've been wondering for some time whether we haven't been on the wrong track altogether."

"Ah?"

"What I mean is that we've been neglecting something.

Something serious, something important. As I see it, we've been overlooking entirely the spiritual aspect of the struggle!"

Mr. Churchill Chan, in the course of an industrious lifetime spent along the highest levels of international diplomacy, had had intimate contact with every known form of greed, duplicity and madness; it was his soft boast, made only to his wife, that no word or deed of the human animal could astonish him. Nevertheless, his old eyes now popped slightly at the use of the unusual word. . . .

"Spiritual?" he echoed. "Ah yes, *spiritual.*" He wondered: another betrayal?

"America," said Christopher, "at the present time is a profoundly spiritual nation. All our best-selling books are about religion: *Peace of Soul, Peace of Mind,* and a good many others. As a matter of fact, I'm told that the country's number-one writer from the point of view of sales is a monk. And in my own case, one of my most popular lectures had to do with two great spiritual leaders: Gandhi and Christ."

"Men of greatness, without doubt." Puzzled, attempting to anticipate these queer, oblique, typically Occidental turns of mind, Mr. Churchill Chan said tentatively, "The Republic of China, although not a Christian nation, has ever been most friendly to Christianity. I myself have a relation, a very fine young man, who is a Methodist. A Methodist-*Episcopal,* I believe. . . ."

"Well, I wasn't thinking in terms of Christianity, precisely; I want to put the whole thing on a broader basis than that. I'll tell you my idea, Mr. Chan. I want," he said, his voice rising, his head ducking and feinting slightly with the words, as though the old Oriental head confronting him had suddenly dissolved into a microphone, "to put it on the basis of a humble people, a religious people, fighting for their traditional beliefs against an atheistic enemy! In other words, I want to interest the people of the United States in a spiritual crusade for China!"

Light dawned, alarmingly. "Prayers," said Mr. Churchill Chan, with a perceptible dullness of tone. "The Republic of China, one does not need to say, would be profoundly grateful for the prayers of the American people. Still, this detestable age in which we live is one of materialism; perhaps assistance of a more material nature would—"

"What I had in mind," Christopher said, "was not so much prayers as the arousing of public indignation to the point where the government would be forced to send planes—"

"AHA!"

"—for the purpose of dropping leaflets, reminding the Chinese people of what they're fighting for, and letting them know that we're with them with all our heart and soul. You know, I think that might provide just the spark that's needed to light the flame!"

"Yes. Well, it is excellent, most excellent. Still," said Mr. Churchill Chan, "one must husband one's resources;

it is a law of existence. How good it would be, then, if these aircraft could perform a dual function. How good it would be if they could be supplied with both leaflets and bombs. . . ."

"No," said Christopher thoughtfully. "No, I hardly think that would be necessary. I think that the propaganda alone would be more effective, in this case. As I see it," he said, "it's fundamentally a problem of awakening a dormant people to what's happening to everything they hold most dear."

"Yes, yes, that is most astute. Still, there is of course the factor of literacy to consider; so few of these people are able to read, therefore the effects of the leaflets would be minimized . . ."

"Picture books," Christopher said, snapping his fingers. "It's a simple matter to dramatize the spiritual struggle in clear, easy to grasp, cartoon form. It's a method we use in this country for instructing our backward children."

"Yes, all excellent. Yet one cannot help but feel that this splendid plan would find even greater success if implemented by a few mere *tokens* of physical authority: bombs, tanks, guns. . . ."

Mr. Churchill Chan fought on with all the doggedness permitted to one in his essentially conciliatory position. It was all to no avail, for Christopher was talking, already drawing up the blueprint for the all-out, airborne crusade (the great planes sweeping in from the sea, buzzing rice paddies, hill, vast and dusty plains; he saw an oppressed peasantry raising hopeful eyes as high above downy-faced American bombardiers prepared to loose precious cargoes of Confucius Comic Books), and while he talked the bland and desperate words of his companion came to him as an indistinct and rather purposeless buzz, of which he was barely aware, and to which he did not attend. When, finally, he showed Mr. Churchill Chan, shrouded in weary smiles, out of the office, he felt that it had been a most productive talk, that once again, out of the free and friendly interchange of opinion and idea, had come clarity of resolution.

Before plunging back into the heavy tide of routine, Christopher went to the office of Adam Flair, on another floor of the building.

"Adam, I'd like to talk to you for a minute."

"Come in, Christopher," said Adam sadly. He was the executive vice-president of the radio network over which Christopher broadcast; he was a man of ability and importance. It was here, in the surprisingly spartan surroundings of his private office, that the really *big* deceptions, deals and purges were born. Adam himself was pale and mournful-eyed, a man in his middle years but of a deceptively youthful appearance. This was of some advantage in an industry which lived in pathological fear of being no longer considered "a young man's game." He was by temperament nongregarious; on the rare evenings when he was free of business pressure, he went home and directly to bed, where, propped up in a nest of pillows, he listened with distaste to the entertainment for which he was in large part responsible. He listened as long as was consistent with duty; then, with a sigh, he snapped the radio off and read himself to sleep in the lonely valleys of Schopenhauer. He was not a particularly happy man.

Christopher liked and respected Adam; it was his entirely mistaken belief that Adam liked and respected him.

"Adam, when are we going to talk about my contract renewal? Has the date been set?"

Adam's face grew more melancholy. Because of his intimate association with those in the broadcasting industry, he had acquired an understandable aversion for human speech; because he was an executive in that industry, there were certain parts of that speech which affected him more adversely than others: words such as "contract renewal," "bonus arrangement," "living wage" . . .

He shut his eyes and said, "No definite date. It all depends on when Udolpho gets back from Europe. I should say Wednesday or Thursday of next week."

Christopher nodded agreeably, rose, and began to stroll about the room, inspecting with great care the worthless objects with which Adam had chosen to surround himself. "Naturally," he said, "naturally, it all depends upon Udolpho." Mr. Bernie Udolpho was the president of Agrarian Products, Incorporated, parent company of the concern that sponsored Christopher's broadcasts. "But I don't anticipate any difficulty with him. He's a bit crude, but he's reasonable. He's always been thoroughly reasonable in the past."

Adam, recognizing the signs, said wearily, "you're going to ask him for more money."

"I think I will, yes," Christopher said, halting his tour of the room, and turning to Adam with a look that invited openness between equals. "And I think I'll get it without any trouble. I'm not greedy, Adam; you know that. But you also know that I have a pretty good idea of my own market value."

"Yes, Christopher, I know."

Christopher began the process of self-assessment. "I'm not an intellectual," he said, with satisfaction. "I've never pretended to be. There are a lot of answers I may not know and probably never will know. But I don't happen to think that matters worth a damn, Adam. What does matter is that I know the *important* things: I know what's right and what's wrong; I know human nature; and I know enough about the world and what makes it tick to talk sense about it every night in the week, Monday through Friday, to five million people. Any way you look at that, it's not small potatoes, Adam!"

Leaning back in his chair, Adam swung around and stared dreamily through the windows out into the autumn afternoon. "Everybody wants more money," he said. "Why?" A morning spent with the representative of three different employees' unions had made him unusually

philosophical upon the point. "*I* don't want more money,"
he said. "Why does everybody else?"

"I don't know about everybody else," Christopher said,
"but with me it's a matter of simple justice." He proceeded
to offer the evidence in support of his claims: the results
of a nation-wide popularity poll, statistics furnished by a
radio-audience survey, the volume of mail he received each
day, and finally, the mounting sales curve of Agrarian
Products, Incorporated.

"So what it really comes down to," he concluded, "is
this: either I'm worth more money or I'm not. Now, you
tell me, Adam: in the face of all the evidence, can Udolpho
honestly say I'm not? What do you think?"

Squinting into the sunlight, Adam said, "I think that
you're crazy to ask for more money."

Christopher made a sound of exasperation. "But why?
Give me one good reason!"

Adam sighed and swung back from the autumn afternoon, back to the bare little office, back to Christopher.
"I can think of more reasons for people not to ask for
money," he said, "than I can for almost anything else I
know. But in your case I'll narrow it down: it's because
I don't think you have a chance of getting it, and because
in all probability you'll get hurt in the attempt."

"I don't see where that follows at all. The point is that
I'm not asking for anything outrageous; I'm asking for a
raise that's entirely justified by the facts!"

"Justified," echoed Adam, nodding. "Your trouble is
one of vocabulary, Christopher; you're using the wrong

words. Words like 'worth' and 'deserving' and 'justified.' You're not going up for a merit badge; you're asking a man to give you a slice of his income. It's never a question of whether you're worth it or not; if it were, almost no one in radio would have a job. The question is, does he want to give it to you? Or better still, are you in a position to *make* him give it to you? Think that over in relation to Udolpho and see what answer you get."

Christopher shook his head. "You're too cynical, Adam. But actually, even arguing it from your point of view, the fact is that I'm in a strong bargaining position."

"You're impregnable," said Adam morosely. "Everybody in this business is in the same strong position; that's why the valley below is littered with bones." He went on to talk with some relish of the men of stature, former associates, who had tumbled through avarice, and now, pitiable and broken, were reduced to seeking employment in Omaha or Des Moines.

"Here's a tip for you, Christopher. You're a great one for talking about Providence in your broadcasts; just for once follow your own advice and don't fly in the face of it. Right now you're sitting on top of the world; why jostle yourself? *Status quo*, Christopher, *status quo*."

"There's nothing wrong with the *status quo*," said Christopher, rising and walking over toward the door, "except that it doesn't pay enough. You're a pessimist, Adam; you don't even like to *think* there's a bright side to things. But I'm not. I'm an optimist; I think that most people get what's coming to them, and I think that right now more money's coming to me. And I'll tell you why: because I understand Udolpho. He's the kind of man who respects results and I have some pretty fair results to show him: five million consumers listening to me every night. I don't think of them as so many consumers, but he does: five million of them. You can't laugh that off, Adam."

"I'm not a merry man," said Adam, "and I can't afford to laugh at incongruities; I make my living from them. All right, Christopher, you've got yourself a pistol. Now here's a final piece of advice: don't fire it. Don't even aim it. Put it down."

Christopher smiled; the brief talk had been heartening, therapeutic. Even now, at this stage of his career, there came rare moments when, about to take an important step, he felt the faint stirrings of irresolution. At such times he consulted others, told them of his plans; in their invariable opposition he saw the confirmation of his own essential rightness.

Opening the door, he said, "You're all wrong, Adam. I respect your judgment, but on this matter, you're all wrong. Believe me, I *know*."

He went out; Adam's secretary came in. She was a handsome, efficient girl with the knowing, rather disdainful manner of young women who type confidential memoranda. She had heard the talk between Christopher and her employer, for Adam took the thoughtful precaution of recording all conversations with his friends. Turning slightly toward the door, she gave it a look of studied contempt; it was a much-admired patrician mannerism which she had copied from the well-bred roles of Miss Barbara Stanwyck.

"Personally," she said, sitting down, "I think he's the world's biggest jerk."

Adam looked at her desolately. "It's these little touches of refinement that really make the day for me," he said. "The gentle tide of Katherine Gibbs lapping away at the shore. Have you brought your book in?"

Ignoring the question, the secretary said, "Well, do you like him?"

"Christopher? No," said Adam, with a little shudder. "No, I don't. But then, I know him, you see, and it's perhaps Christopher's greatest advantage that he's disliked only by the people who know him. He has five million listeners, almost none of whom know him, and with them he's wildly successful. I find that fact impressive."

The secretary sniffed. "If you ask me," she said, "they're five million morons."

"It's the basest ingratitude for anyone in this business to sneer at morons," Adam said severely. "Never have so few owed so much to so many. Radio is the truest form of democracy: one moron with a little spending money is equal to Albert Einstein any day. As for Christopher, he's captured their hearts, and they've captured his; they feed on each other's flesh, and both wax fat. At the moment, Christopher is preparing to wax a little fatter."

The secretary's pretty red lips curved in a smile of anticipation. "That's what I'm waiting for," she said. "When he asks for more money."

"Daydreams, little girl," sighed Adam. "Pure wishful thinking. When he asks for more money, he'll get it, or at least I'm fairly certain he will. There's really no reason why Udolpho shouldn't come across. He's a tough little ape, but he's had a very good year, and it was a year for which Christopher was partially responsible. No, forget the happy thoughts; the grim fact is that Christopher will come through with the usual flying colors."

Disappointed, she said: "But you said—"

"Yes, I said. The trouble is that Christopher didn't believe me. I'm against Christopher's getting more money, for several reasons. One, the network will receive not one red cent from any increase incurring to Christopher in talent fees; as we are an organization depending upon annual revenue, we understandably lack some of Christopher's enthusiasm for his project. Two, any salary demand, even a reasonable one, can tie up contract negotiations forever, and I'm not anxious to spend long hours closeted with Bernie Udolpho all for the greater prosperity of Christopher Usher. And finally," he said thoughtfully, "I must confess I'm not particularly eager to see a richer, healthier, happier Christopher around the premises; he's difficult enough as it is. Now if you have no objections, we'll forget Christopher and get down to work."

The secretary assumed the attitude of elegant aloofness so necessary to the taking of dictation. "Personally," she said, "I *still* say he's a jerk. . . ."

Humming contentedly, Christopher walked back to his office. On the way, he remembered that an important phone call was yet to be made; prudence directed him to a pay-phone booth. He had to cancel an appointment for that evening; it was a cancellation which he now regretted having to make, and it was a cancellation which was not received with the best of grace.

"Sometimes," Lura pouted, "I think you don't even consider my feelings at all."

"Now don't talk like that, Lura; you know that isn't so. It's just that I'm caught in one of those evenings: the theater, an after-theater party, and that kind of thing. I have to go; you can appreciate that in my position I have to be reasonably careful . . ."

"Careful," said Lura, in a voice of tragedy. "I'm so tired of being careful, Chris. Do you know what I feel like doing right now? I feel just like going out and standing on the rooftops and shouting: 'Yes, I love my Chris baby and he loves me!' That's how I feel, Chris!"

"Now, now!" he said, alarmed. "You're a sensible girl, Lura; you don't want to think of such rash things." He was puzzled and disturbed by these occasional bursts of gypsy fervor, which occurred unpredictably, and in broad daylight; possibly, he thought, it was her heritage as an actress. "I'm very anxious to see you, Lura," he said. "I have some news for you. Good news."

"Chris baby! You didn't go ahead and buy me that present! Such a thoughtful man!"

"You're going to have all the presents your heart desires," Christopher said, slipping easily into the old-fashioned language of romantic promise. "I discussed my new contract demands with the network today and I'm presenting them to a sponsor next week. I'll tell you all about it tomorrow night. That is," he said, a trifle slyly, "if you're going to be in."

"Mmmm," said Lura. "*Mmmm!*"

Back in the office, there were new piles of dispatches, late flashes from an active world, additional grist to the mill. Christopher glanced at them briefly, for it was time for his afternoon nap. This was the one hiatus, the solitary period of refreshment, his self-imposed regimen allowed. It was a long one, lasting a little better than two hours. He slept easily, his rest abetted by a parade of satisfactory dreams. Wonderful scenes shot across his slumbers with dazzling rapidity; infinitely varied, they were connected only in their common central figure:

He saw himself in a vast and gloomy hall where he had never been before. A door had closed behind him; a dozen silent, frozen-faced men in drab uniforms cut off the possibility of withdrawal. Suddenly the great double doors on the opposite side of the hall swept open: a small man—surprisingly small—with stiff graying hair, a graying mustache, his left arm held close to his side, came slowly across to him. "You are the only man of your country," said Stalin, in an English painfully acquired for the occasion, "with whom I will consent to talk. . . ."

. . . in an outrigger canoe, shooting along over a sea of astonishing blue; in the prow, kneeling, a woman, bronzed and gloriously nubile. "Whee!" cried Lura. "Whee, Chris baby, the water's just like *sapphires.* . . ."

. . . in a small, intimate room of a renovated mansion in the capital of the nation, a room seldom visited by civilians. He was alone with a man of decidedly worried appearance. "Let's call off this senseless feud," pleaded the President of the United States. . . .

. . . in the middle of an extraordinary negotiation. "What I got in mind," said Mr. Udolpho, "is you should get a piece of the profits on *everything* we sell. . . ."

. . . on a balcony, a little like the Pope in Rome, addressing the throng below. He was speaking of kittens; from time to time there came the great, punctuating roars of "Usher! Usher!" Those who did not roar sobbed unashamedly. . . .

When he awoke, he felt remarkably fit, and he wrote his broadcast in no time at all. . . .

That night, at the theater, Meredith told him of the expected arrival of General Blackburn. Christopher was delighted, but not to the point of sharing information. For the moment, he decided not to tell his wife of his proposed salary demands.

three

THE FOLLOWING WEEK WAS A PERIOD OF EXCITEMENT, OF
arrival. On Monday, Christopher learned that Mr. Bernie
Udolpho had returned from his European tour, and that
the contract talks had been assigned to Thursday. But
this was not all; twenty-four hours before the scheduled
conference, Christopher and Meredith drove out to the
airport to greet an old acquaintance.

The plane roared down from cloudless skies and came
to a throbbing halt. In the gleaming side a door popped
open prematurely, revealing a lone, martial figure hastily
scrambling into a position of photogenic alertness. He
stood for a moment: trim, elegant, expectant; then, as

there were neither cheers nor flashing bulbs, he strode to the strains of inaudible marches down the ladder and across the concrete runway. Like Napoleon approaching the coast at Antibes, like MacArthur wading through Pacific surf, General Walter "Beak" Blackburn was returning. His step firm, his fine old warrior's head—as yet unravaged by wound or thought—held high, he was returning from his inspection of the historic and disused forts of Southern California.

"Home is where the heart is," he said, smiling benignly at Christopher and Meredith. "Is it possible that you have a bunk for a weary old soldier?"

That night, at the dinner table, the general gave no sign of weariness. He talked freely and at great length of impressions gathered on his latest tour.

"The country is in excellent shape," he said. In the full serenity of his advanced years, he had acquired the bland, detached speech of the elder statesman. Gracefully, authoritatively, ceaselessly, his simple-minded pronouncements poured out like a river of velvet, and all the while he talked, he ate. He ate enormously and beautifully, fingers, hands, wrists and elbows co-operating in a series of movements so symphonic as to almost conceal the progress of an epic gluttony.

"Excellent shape," he said. "In all my years, I've never known it to be better. Morale is high, people are truly singing as they toil. I wonder if I might have just a bit more of this delicious beef, Meredith. That rather rare piece will do very nicely; ah, thank you, my dear, thank you. Yes, when people ask me to describe the mood of our country today, I like to do it in one word: *confident!*"

"I couldn't agree with you more," said Christopher. "As you know, General, it's a point I've been stressing on my broadcasts for years."

"Oh yes. And speaking of your broadcasts, Christopher, I wonder if you begin to realize the remarkable effect they're having upon West Coast thinking." Momentarily abandoning his fork, the general gestured gracefully in the direction of the thinking West. "Simply remarkable," he said. "I saw signs of it on every side."

Christopher made a becoming movement of self-depreciation. "I hope they have some influence," he said. "It's true that I'm carried on quite a number of stations out there."

"You are not only heard on the widest possible scale," said the general, "but what is more important, you are heard *by the people who count*. I am thinking particularly of the film capital; there your audience is of the highest caliber, Christopher. Do you by any chance know a man named Thompson? Tugger Thompson?"

"*Tugger* Thompson?" Christopher said doubtfully. "No, I don't believe I do."

"That's not the cowboy-picture man?" Meredith asked. "The one who sings to his horse?"

The general beamed at her. "Yes, my dear, I believe he has appeared principally in films of the Old West," he said, "although he informs me that he is soon to be featured in a remarkable religious picture; as I remember it, he is to be St. Paul. We became fast friends in the course of my stay, for in addition to being a splendid actor, he's an exceptionally sound thinker. However, to come to the point of my little story. One evening last week I happened to be present at a large and gala party, given by the National Guard. And at one point in the evening, when a good many of the young people were in the ballroom, laughing and dancing and in general having a good time, Tugger and myself and other more mature spirits were gathered about the radio listening to Christopher's broadcast. It was well done, of course, unusually well done, and as it came to its conclusion, Tugger rose slowly to his feet and said, in tones of utmost sincerity: 'There, in my opinion, is the one man who talks good sense more consistently than any other man in America today!' Needless to say, my dear Christopher, the entire room was in substantial agreement." He leaned back and regarded his host; in a curiously absent-minded manner, he reached for the green beans. "I'm afraid I may have embarrassed you," he said, twinkling, "but you must allow an old friend these occasional pleasures."

Christopher smiled, weathering embarrassment well. It was Meredith who, with an uttered doubt, restored the conversation to the less restricted field of national affairs.

"You think, then, General, that people are confident in spite of things like the hydrogen bomb?"

"Not in spite of them, my dear; *because* of them." He smiled cryptically at her; it was the smile of the high-level insider. "There are those of us who believe," he said, "that the so-called H-Bomb would be our greatest guarantee of peace."

"Yes, that's what Christopher says. But so many of the scientists don't seem to agree."

"You listen to your husband, my dear," advised the general. "When you've reached my age, you'll realize that scientists are all very well in their way, but they're hardly qualified to express opinions on military matters. Let them stay in their laboratories and leave the business of national security to those of us who are just a bit more familiar with the problem. *Pickled watermelon rind!*" he exclaimed, with an air of delighted discovery. "Thank you so much, my dear. I've always believed," he said, "that these little spiced accessories spell the difference between a merely good meal and a feast!"

Christopher, not altogether pleased by the faintly traitorous line of his wife's questioning, returned to the hydrogen bomb. "The trouble with women on something like this," he said, rather irritably, "is that they're apt to lose their heads. Now as I see it, we need to look at this with just a little common sense. First of all, will the bomb ever be used? I doubt it; I doubt it extremely. Any aggressor would fear retaliation, and that's what I mean by saying it's our greatest safeguard for peace. But let's suppose, for the sake of argument, that somebody, in the distant future, *should* decide to use it. And let's suppose it should be used against us. All right: are we going to spend our lives in fear and trembling because of a remote possibility? Are we going to dig caves and drive our civilization underground? I say we need to be sensible; I say that what we need to do first is to realize that the hydrogen bomb is still just a *weapon*. A big weapon, yes, but still a weapon."

"In other words," said Meredith, "terrible, but not so terrible."

"No, that's not it at all," said Christopher, who rather resented the simplification of his own words, particularly when he suspected a perversion of his meaning. "What I am saying is that there's no reason to think the world is coming to an end simply because a new weapon may be produced. We've had new weapons before," he said, appealing to history. "Every weapon ever used in warfare was once a new weapon, and every one of them was supposed to mean the end of mankind, but what happened? I'll tell you what happened: for every weapon, there was a defense. Sometimes these defenses weren't perfect, but at least they were always good enough to stop all this nonsense about 'invincible weapons.' So I don't intend to go into a panic because of the atomic bomb or the hydrogen bomb or any other kind of bomb. I look at these things in the light of what's happened in the past, and I hope I have enough faith in American ingenuity to believe that anything we've devised we can certainly protect ourselves against!"

"How right you are!" said the general. "I well recall the feeling of public consternation which greeted the first appearance of the airship in a military role." He launched into an affectionate anecdote of the aviation horrors of World War I, studding his story with the names and details of primal, almost-forgotten aircraft, lumbering across European skies: Handley-Paiges, Spads, Fokkers, Gothas, Sopwiths, Nieuports, Caproni triplanes. "And then," he said, "to restore public confidence, along came the anti-aircraft guns! I remember the French Archies as being particularly good. All of which," he concluded, "supports the wisdom of Christopher's position, and also brings us to the conclusion that despite all our wonderful advances, *every war must still be fought and won on the ground.* The humble doughboy is still king; that is a fact I never tire of impressing upon our newly enlisted men. It seems to do wonders for their morale; I wish you could see their faces as they listen to my words!"

Meredith, with some persistence, said, "Then you think, along with Christopher, that we would have a defense against this bomb?"

"Oh, yes, yes, without a doubt, my dear. Between ourselves, it is constantly being talked of in G.H.Q."

"Well then, what is it?"

A look of extraordinary solemnity crossed the fine old features. "That, my dear, I am not at liberty to discuss even here," he said, "save to say that it has *something to do with zinc.* But what is this?" he cried, an enraptured eye falling upon a tray freshly produced from the kitchen. "French pastry! Meredith, how good of you to remember an old soldier's weakness; the perfect climax to an incomparable meal!"

The dinner over, they moved into the library, and there, the consolations of the table being denied him, the general sought solace in increased volubility. Christopher kept pace with him. Often, both men talked at once on quite unallied subjects; it was the sort of conversation possible only to good companions whose high regard for each other is tempered by the stronger power of self-absorption. As the night wore on, the general retreated more deeply into the past, dredging from fond memory the mnemonics of magnificence: Wipers, Verdun, Black Jack Pershing, Sir Douglas Haig, the Rose of No Man's Land. From time to time Christopher returned him to the present, hoping to probe behind the veil of military secrecy; in reply the general smiled elliptically and violated in great detail the confidences of thirty years before. Fortunately, as Christopher was not really listening, it made small difference.

It was much later when Meredith, almost unobserved, slipped out of the room. The two men remained talking for an hour or more. As, at last, they prepared to retire, Christopher told the general of the financial demands which he intended to make the next afternoon. The general smiled sadly.

"You're very wise, Christopher. You are reaping the rewards of leadership; you will be receiving that which is your due. It so seldom happens that proper recognition is bestowed upon those who most deserve it," the general sighed. "I rarely speak of personal injustice, and yet there have been times when, looking about me, I have felt that Fortune has somehow passed me by. I am not speaking of money: an old bachelor like myself has little use for worldly goods. And undoubtedly there is a great reward simply in reviewing all the good work one has done. Still, I suspect that the greatest honors have eluded me. I sometimes wonder if my work will survive me. Will there be, I wonder, even *posthumous* recognition?"

Christopher clapped him comfortingly on the shoulder. "You're taking the gloomy view of things, General; you're too modest. You've earned your niche in history."

"I hope so," said the old man. "Still, things so seldom work out as they should."

"Incidentally," said Christopher, "it might be just as well if you didn't mention anything about this salary business to Meredith. I thought I wouldn't tell her just yet."

"Of course," said the general, sensing chivalry. "I understand fully, Christopher. These matters are always best left to the menfolk; then, once accomplished, they can be revealed as the happy surprises that they are."

"Yes, that's it exactly. And now, if you're ready, I think we can turn in."

"Lead on," said the general, with a little flourish of his hand. A quotation, imperfectly mastered in the long-ago years of his youth, now came startlingly to mind; it was

62

military, in a way, and singularly apposite to the moment. "Lead on, MacDuff," said the general happily; "may flocks of angels see thee to thy rest. . . ."

The conference did not take place in Adam's private office, but in one of the more sumptuous parlors reserved for the reception of valued clients. Shortly before the scheduled hour, Christopher, Adam, and Adam's secretary were joined by Jason Rooney. He was the president of the advertising agency which represented Agrarian Products: a large, pink man who looked like a well-barbered pig. His professional standing was of the highest: he had a formal pomposity of manner and speech, and could, when things went his way, shed a fraudulent radiance over most gatherings of which he was a part.

"Adam, Christopher, Miss deVries," he said, bowing, and rubbing plump hands together briskly. "All assembled to greet our returning voyager, I see. Well, well. I hope this beautiful day is a sign of good fortune for us all." In a deft, unbroken flow of movement, he slid from his fawn-colored topcoat, fluffed up the carnation on his lapel, pressed cigarettes into the hands of the others, and folded smoothly into a chair, simultaneously centering the incredible creases of his trousers. This accomplished, he leaned back and regarded his companions with a look of immense shrewdness.

"Um, yes," he said, blowing a circlet of smoke. "Yes *indeed.*"

Adam looked at Christopher. "You haven't changed your mind, I suppose?"

"No, no. You'll see, Adam: everything will work out very well."

"In point of fact," said Jason Rooney, "as I anticipate—correctly, I trust—that this will be a routine renewal, I mentioned to Mr. Udolpho that there was really no necessity of his attending. However, you know as well as I how he feels about maintaining personal contacts; I think we may expect him shortly."

"He'll be glad he came," said Adam.

Precisely on time, Mr. Bernie Udolpho arrived. He entered the room silently, almost hesitantly.

"Hullo," he said, in a soft and rather hoarse voice. "Everybody's here, huh?"

Mr. Udolpho was diminutive, round, swarthy, Sicilian, and a millionaire. More than twenty-five years ago, in the atmosphere of moral conflict which had pervaded his adopted city of Chicago, he had disgraced his family and friends by choosing to operate within the law. It had proved to be the wisest of decisions. As one by one his father, brothers and boyhood chums had gone tumbling into federal penitentiaries, young Bernie had bought up their plants and rolling stock for a song, and had converted them to the wholesome production of restorative salves, oils and jellies. Now the ruler of an intricate empire of vegetable lotions, Mr. Udolpho modestly ascribed his success to his observance of two fundamental rules.

"Do It Legal," he would say, holding up one stubby finger. "It Pays to Advertise," he would conclude, holding up another.

It was from Mr. Udolpho's lavish adherence to this second principle that Christopher had profited handsomely for a number of years.

There was a general exchange of amenities; Mr. Udolpho looked at Adam with soft brown eyes and asked: "You fellas here are doing okay these days?"

"Business isn't too bad, Mr. Udolpho. Not too bad at all." In moments of high negotiation, Adam was curiously transfigured. He shed his cynicism; his manner became frank, eager, almost ingenuous; his boyish face acquired a simple, undergraduate glow. As the crises appeared and deepened, he seemed to grow younger, until finally it was with an appearance of schoolboy embarrassment that he nailed the unwary client to the cross. "We're not having one of our peak years, but the billing is holding up pretty well. Golly, I just hope it continues!"

"Yeh," said Mr. Udolpho. He looked appraisingly at Christopher. "You look good," he said. "Real healthy."

"I feel well, thank you, Mr. Udolpho," Christopher said. "I've been working fairly hard lately, but I've managed to keep in pretty good shape."

"I claim that might well be ascribed to a congenial employment," said Jason Rooney, with a buttery smile. "To an association which has proved of the greatest benefit to us all."

"Yes, of course," said Christopher, with some impatience; it was not through the suety appreciations of Jason Rooney that *his* cause was to be advanced. He hastened to join Adam in the rite of solicitous preliminary: the deferential blend of inquiry and compliment which was the industry's silken approach to cash on the barrelhead.

In this instance, the approach was difficult. Mr. Udolpho lacked the customary passion of the self-made man for elaborate response; he had accumulated too much money by listening to be fond of talking. He contented himself with attending politely, at times smiling gently and offering the briefest of replies. Occasionally he picked his teeth. He seemed to be in no hurry.

Discussion passed from the state of Mr. Udolpho's health to the more fertile topic of his odyssey.

"Frankly, I envied you your trip to Europe," Christopher said. Losing sight, for the moment, of his immediate objective, he continued. "I've been wanting to go for the last four years; I've given some thought to going over this spring. I think what I'd really like to do is examine at first-hand the effects of our reconstruction aid. I think—"

Swiftly, Adam said, "What were your impressions of the recovery program, Mr. Udolpho? Are the countries on their way up?"

Mr. Udolpho answered immediately. "It's lousy over there," he said. "They should burn it down and begin all over."

Adam nodded enthusiastically; Christopher, slightly shocked by this callousness toward an area in which he felt a sense of proprietorship, said, "But there must be some areas where our program has done very well. When you speak of failure, Mr. Udolpho, do you have any one country in mind? I mean, that you consider beyond redemption?"

Mr. Udolpho nodded. "Ireland," he said.

Jason Rooney laughed, a little too loudly. "Oh, come now, Mr. Udolpho! I think I should warn you that Mr. Usher may be taking your little joke seriously!"

"Joke," said Mr. Udolpho; a curious brooding expression crept into his eyes. "Three days I got stranded there," he said, "in the rain." After a pause he added, "I hate bacon."

With an exuberance appropriate to the stage of negotiations, Adam said, "Golly, what a time you must have had!"

"Yeh," said Mr. Udolpho. "Yeh." Then, suddenly and surprisingly, prompted by unfathomable impulse, he told the story of contemporary Europe in a few blunt sentences. From this story emerged a Europe which would have been unrecognizable to even the most experienced traveler, for, with an admirable disregard for inessentials, Mr. Udolpho divorced the continent from all historical, military, ethical, or human associations. He had seen Europe through the highly selective eye of an exporter of nose drops and skin foods; padding about amid the glories of the western world, moving with apparent freedom behind the Iron Curtain, he had watched alertly for the incidence of acne, catarrh, and falling hair. He had traveled swiftly and widely; frontiers had meant nothing, for the sebaceous gland was everywhere. He had witnessed the disintegration of pride in personal appearance; he had seen the emergence of inferior, home-grown products; he realized at the completion of his tour, that he had seen a ruined market.

He told this story in a manner which was quiet, matter-of-fact, free from acrimony. It was the simple, dehumanized report of a sensible man who has learned to accept the bitter with the sweet. Christopher listened with a scarcely suppressible indignation: this dismal land of scurf and scale was not *his* Europe! But he listened also with uncertainty, for in the year that had elapsed since their last meeting, he had forgotten Mr. Udolpho's peculiar limitations. A problem presented itself: from exactly what angle did one approach the question of a fair wage with a man who saw the living western world in terms of a vast epidermis? He was still pondering this when Mr. Udolpho, glancing casually at the slim timepiece on his wrist, brought his dissertation to a close.

"Okay," he said. With a tired flutter of his eyelids, he blinked a continent out of mind; folding pudgy brown hands across a broad vest, he got down to the business of the day. "So now what?" he inquired.

Jason Rooney magically produced a bundle of documents, apparently whisking them out of the air. "I've always found the agreeable experiences of the past well worth repeating," he said, smiling wisely. "And I don't think that any of us here are prepared to say that our relationship during the past year has not been thoroughly agreeable. It would be difficult to imagine a more satisfactory arrangement. It was my thought, then, that we might proceed on that basis."

Adam, without looking at Christopher, spoke quickly, and in the best tradition of the playing field. "Why, that sounds all right to me," he said. "The network wants to be fair about this: if you're satisfied, I don't see why we shouldn't be. I think it would be swell if we could keep on just the way we've been going!"

"My thought exactly," smiled Jason Rooney, extending the papers. "Well then, perhaps, in view of—"

"Wait," commanded Mr. Udolpho. Veteran of a thousand similar moments, witness of long skirmishes on the seasoned battlefield of his purse, he had a feel for the potential stand-off; he looked thoughtfully at Christopher. "You ain't said nothing," he pointed out.

It was an opening, generously provided, and casting doubts aside, Christopher leaped. "I don't agree with what's been said," he said. "Altogether, that is. While I have enjoyed doing my work, I think that under any new contract, some adjustments should be made, in all fairness to me."

In an abrupt maneuver of dissociation, Adam said, "Adjustments, Christopher?"

"Well, well, well!" Jason Rooney said. "This represents something of a surprise, at least to me. It seems that in the light of what Mr. Udolpho has just said, Christopher, any new demands would be out—"

"Shh," said Mr. Udolpho, cutting him off with a peremptory wave. He nodded, not unamiably, to Christopher. "Go ahead," he said. "You got something to say, let's hear it."

Christopher talked. At home in the bracing climate of the monologue, he talked in the full perfection of his broadcast style. He talked, not to an audience of millions, but to an audience of one, silent, olive-skinned man who listened impassively, now and then plucking at his lower lip with a stubby thumb and forefinger. Christopher's argument was an elaboration of that which he had presented to Adam the week before; it was rooted in the demonstrable fact that Usher was booming. He discussed himself with candor, eloquence and passion. There was the growth of his radio popularity, scientifically established; there were the personal appearances, the lecture tours, the ever-mounting importance of the personal, good-will ambassador; and there were the new avenues, so recently explored: his broadcasts, for example, were now being recorded and played back during the daytime hours, as compulsory listening, in the public schools of three large cities—Usher was contacting youth, the funnel to the parent, the consumer of tomorrow.

The appeal for reward commensurate with achievement was thus presented on the highest possible plane. Only at the end did Christopher hint—and then most delicately—of a volatile public, a market easily swayed, of five million consumers following their pied piper in a regretful but necessary desertion of their favorite nasal salve. It was here that Mr. Udolpho showed his only sign of emotion. A slight smile touched his lips; it was this form of subtle blackjack that made him think of home. His head bobbed in perfect comprehension.

"Okay," he said simply. "How much?"

Christopher told him, quickly; Jason Rooney drew in a sharp breath of protest. "A great surprise to me," he said, his pink pork face alive with reproach. "I think it's ridiculous to—"

"Shh," said Mr. Udolpho again. "Don't talk." He looked speculatively at Adam. "You in on this?" he asked.

Adam shook his head; the boyish face looked older, warier. "The network is satisfied," he said briefly. "This is Christopher's pitch."

Mr. Udolpho nodded, rose slowly, and walked over to one of the windows. He stood there for some time, staring reflectively into outside space, one foot tapping in rhythmic tempo on the thick carpet. No one spoke. Christopher watched him carefully; solemnly aware that the negotiations had narrowed to a duel of two large and equal personalities, he stared as though seeking some faint clue to decision in the broad little back. He was confident, for he knew that he had right on his side, that he had, moreover, put his case well; he would have been still more confident if the back confronting him had not been so sturdy, so intractable. . . .

Mr. Udolpho turned abruptly. "That's a lotta dough," he stated. He spoke directly to Christopher; oddly enough, he looked almost jolly. "No kidding," he said, "you really think I'm gonna give you that kinda dough?" He motioned toward Adam and Jason Rooney. "Look at them," he said. "They're smart fellas. You think *they* think I'm gonna give it to you?"

Christopher did not need to look; conscious of heroic loneliness, he said, "I'm not interested in what they think. *I* think it's a sound business proposition. The only thing that really counts now is what *you* think."

Mr. Udolpho chuckled hoarsely. "Yeh," he said. "Yeh, that's right. Okay, you wanna know what I think, I'll tell you." Christopher saw the soft brown eyes examine him with the meditative stare of a butcher weighing meat. "I ain't made up my mind," said Mr. Udolpho. "Not yet. Maybe, maybe not. I dunno." He looked at Christopher for a moment more; then he turned, walked back to his chair, and picked up his coat. "I ain't made up my mind," he said again. "No hurry." To Jason Rooney he said, "Come on."

Jason Rooney rose in alert obedience, transmitting waves of distress. Adam said quickly, "Now let's see, how does this leave us? You want to postpone all negotiations, Mr. Udolpho?"

"Yeh," said Mr. Udolpho, walking to the door.

For just a fraction of a second, Christopher felt an almost overwhelming urge to shout his willingness to compromise; he stifled it and said, "When can I expect to hear from you? Or would you rather have me contact you?"

"When I make up my mind," said Mr. Udolpho, "I'll ring you up. So long." And he left, with Jason Rooney trailing in a silent, fussy wake.

"Well, Christopher, I saw," Adam said slowly. "If that's what you wanted me to see. I saw it. You're lucky you're still alive."

Christopher heard him only imperfectly. He was not interested in the premature, somewhat menacing withdrawal of a client; he was interested in first causes. He reviewed in detail the events which had crowded the past few minutes; he heard again his every word, pounding with unstayable force against the formidable little rock of Udolpho. It was only as these words returned to him in totality, as the relentless mosaic of his own spoken logic took shape in his recollection, that he realized just how superb he had been. Confidence grew like a great, benign weed, strangling doubt; in a voice of controlled delight, he said: "Adam, I've got him! I'm as sure of it as I've ever been of anything in my life. He won't give in now because I forced him into a corner, but he's going to give in and he knows it. And what's better, I know it!"

"Congratulations," Adam said. "You're going to fall

right on your tail, but congratulations, if that's what you expect."

"Don't you believe it," Christopher said. With a gay step, he walked to the door through which his opponent of the moment before had left. "Don't you believe it, Adam." With some derision he added, "You were all wrong, Adam; I don't care if you admit it or not, but you were, and you know it!"

After a pause, Adam's secretary said, "Well, now what do you think?"

Adam shrugged. "I think what I've always thought," he said. "He's home free. He got over the hump and the money's as good as in his pocket."

"It didn't look like it to me," she said hopefully.

"Udolpho's a shrewd man," Adam said. "He doesn't like Christopher, and he doesn't like to be held up, but the point is that once he gets home and takes a look at the books, he'll decide that Christopher is a good buy even at the new rate of exchange. No, we can look forward to more talks in about a week," he sighed, "and Christopher can start putting it in the bank right now. Unfortunately, this has been Christopher's day."

Late that night, after listening to a jubilant report, General Walter Blackburn expressed a similar opinion.

"This man Udolpho sounds like an old campaigner to me," he said. "I recognize the strategy, Christopher: one knows one is beaten, but one delays as long as possible, to lend dignity to the final capitulation. In this instance, I think you can look forward to an early settlement, my dear fellow. My heartiest congratulations!"

On a night flight back to the Middle West, a little figure sat wide-awake in the plane, staring thoughtfully ahead, whistling soundlessly at the autumn moon. On matters of this kind, Mr. Bernie Udolpho came to decisions slowly.

four

CHRISTOPHER WAS JUBILANT. HE ALONE HAD FOUGHT THE pitched battle with the formidable monarch of the nasal salves; he alone had won. The realization penetrated his every moment. Each night, now, in his dreams, he sailed through the heady empyrean of his personal triumph, sometimes with Lura, sometimes alone. In the morning, he awoke gently; there was no rude jolt as he slid from sleep into the conscious contemplation of his own increased distinction. As he lay in bed, stretching luxuriously, cracking his joints in a ritual of autochiropractic, he considered the future: he was sure that the tilt with Udolpho had somehow projected him into a larger, more fertile universe, the possibilities of which he could not as yet even imagine. Big things, still to be defined, lay ahead; he knew that, and in the face of almost-Islamic promise he bounded out of bed and, donning his all-rubber exercise garment, began happily to deep-knee bend.

There was the necessity—at least for the moment—of guarding the good news against the speculations of his wife; he realized this and moved with care. Still, temperamentally he was not suited to the concealment of success; his satisfaction was at once detectable in a heightened jauntiness of bearing, an odd, seigneur-like benignity which flowed out toward those about him. Meredith, although accustomed to her husband's radiant spasms of self-content, found herself vaguely puzzled by this present excessive behavior.

"Christopher, you're bubbling with hidden joys!" she observed one night. "What is it? New honors, as yet unannounced? An honorary degree? A secret inheritance? Or what?"

She spoke playfully, but the part about the inheritance had come uncomfortably close to the truth and, for one chilling instant, Christopher wondered if the general had been babbling.

"Ah ha ha ha," he said, patting her on the cheek, sparring for time. "Hidden joys?" He concluded quickly that the general had not talked, that it had been merely the random workings of feminine intuition, so difficult to predict, so startling in its occasional accuracies. "No, no hidden joys," he said. "Not a thing concealed, Meredith;

nothing up my sleeve. If I seem to be happy, I *am*: I'm always happy when I'm busy. And I've been extremely busy lately, Meredith. Busy with Asia: I've been watching it twenty-four hours a day. Something is brewing over there, Meredith; something *big!*" He rubbed his hands together energetically in a gesture appropriate to the mood of the custodian of a continent in ferment. "Keep your eye on Asia," he warned, and inwardly resolved to be more careful in the future.

Circumspection was aided by circumstance, for by the happiest of coincidences, he had been scheduled to leave home that week for another of his ten-day lecture tours—a brisk, productive swing through the Middle West and South. Buoyed by his recent triumph, he was more impatient than usual to get started, to arrive, to know once more the accolade of a vis-à-vis public. He bade a bouncy farewell to his wife and the general; the parting with Lura was more distressing, for she was deeply resentful at being left behind.

"But why *can't* I go? I love to travel *anywhere!*" She lay recumbent on the divan, moodily kicking the zebrine cushions; gaiety and invitation had melted before disappointment, and now her face was wreathed in a childish and rather alarming scowl. "You never take me with you. I think it's because you're ashamed of me. That's what it is: you're *ashamed* of me!" One foot flexed out in a vigorous kick of distemper; a purple pump sailed through the air and thumped against the luminous crucifix on the wall.

"Now I'll have bad luck!" she moaned, burying her face in the pillows. Such was the measure of her wrath that the box of chocolates by her side had not as yet been touched.

In the center of the room, Christopher moved uncertainly back and forth, a vessel of sweet reason, buffeted by these wild, emotional tides. "You're missing the point," he said. "You're missing the whole point, Lura . . ."

"I'm young, I'm *alive!*" she cried, bounding startlingly from the divan. "I'm not asking for much. I just want to go out and dance and have *good times!*" She whirled about in a pirouette to emphasize her youth, vitality, physical flexibility. "You never take me *anywhere*," she said accusingly. "Not even on this *wonderful* little trip!"

"You know I'd love to take you out dancing," Christopher said, somewhat desperately; this was ground that had been covered often before. "Or anywhere else, for that matter. It's not at all a question of not wanting to; it's purely a question of prudence. I have to be careful; I have enemies; no man in my position is without them. And as far as this trip is concerned, surely you can see how dangerous it might be. These people I'm going to talk to are wonderful people, the backbone of the country, the very salt of the earth, but they're deeply conventional. They look up to me, Lura; in many ways they count on me for guidance. If we were, well, *discovered*, so to speak, I might do irreparable harm to that faith. They just wouldn't understand."

"But I understand," Lura said bitterly. "I understand it's all right for me to stay here alone, all because a few hicks with nasty minds might—"

"No," Christopher said sharply. "Not hicks, Lura. Not hicks at all. They may be simple people, they may be the little people, but they're fine people, they're good people. I've told you that before, Lura; I wish you'd remember it."

As if by magic, her resentment dissolved. "Chris *baby*," she sighed. "Lura didn't mean to be bad!" She had gone too far; she knew that Christopher did not relish contemptuous reference to those who were his public. "Chris *baby*," she cooed again, her full lips pouting in appeal, in self-accusation, her voice swinging automatically into the husky accents of enticement. "Chris baby should be *friends* with naughty Lura!"

An inverse Magdalen, naughty Lura approached, sultrily penitent, eager to make amends; disarmed by contrition and the promise of felicitous atonement, Christopher could not help but be stirred to magnanimity. He smiled and gave her an affectionate pinch.

"All right," he said. "All right, Lura. Lura and Chris will be friends."

It was in the consolations of such a friendship that all tensions vanished, that talk turned gradually from the terms of soft endearment to instruction on world affairs and then, quite naturally, to the mention of precious stones. Christopher left for the West supremely contented;

in the entire and intricate pattern of his personal and professional affairs, he could find not so much as a solitary flaw.

At home, in the course of rearranging the helpful light gymnastic apparatus in Christopher's bedroom, Meredith had come upon his scrapbooks. She had read them many times before; she knew that even now he took great pride in keeping them *au courant*, clipping and pasting away with a yeasty vigor which the years had failed to diminish. They were great, plump volumes, dating back to the immediate postcollege years, and filled to the bursting with newsprint and photographs. Because it was possible that an imperishable record of one man's growth and achievement might one day be of some public interest, he had taken the precaution of having them handsomely bound. Now, once more, Meredith flipped back through the layers of her husband's career. It was not until midway in the "Aug. '40-Apr. '41" volume that the sharp dichotomy occurred: quite suddenly, pictures and stories combined in vivid proof that one way of life had died, that another had been born. Quite suddenly, the pictures of Christopher posed in amiable combination with such specialized figures as Dizzy Dean, Connie Mack, Potsy Clark, Willie Hoppe and Whirlaway came abruptly to an end; they were succeeded by a photographic sequence which had become progressively impressive with the passage of time: Christopher dining with the governor of Nebraska; Christopher shaking hands with the Haitian ambassador; Christopher in baccalaureate garb, receiving an honorary doctorate from a theological school in the South; Christopher smiling at Jim Farley; Christopher on the Dewey train; Christopher stalking from the press gallery at a UNESCO meeting; Christopher at a brotherhood banquet, flanked by Mrs. Roosevelt and Eddie Cantor; Christopher alone before the microphone, looking wise, irradiated, willing to share. . . .

Meredith, thumbing through familiar pages, smiled slightly: in each of the pictures, a hint of the faintly preposterous traced its way, the unmistakable signature. More thoughtfully, she regarded a strange, irregular chain of similar and rather obscure clippings, stretched out across the years: in themselves, they appeared to be without relevance to Christopher or his work, yet it was these alone which embraced the two careers, which had spanned the otherwise unbridgeable fissure. These clippings dealt with a single topic: the anonymous and liberal donations of food, clothing or money to the needy. The meticulous inclusion of such notices in the scrapbooks indicated perhaps that Christopher had no serious objection to a posthumous recognition of his good deeds; nevertheless, it remained a source of constant surprise to his wife that never, since their marriage, had he boasted, and seldom had he spoken, of them. It was a queer, inconsonant quirk for which Meredith could forgive him much; as she looked now through the long list, she smiled again, more softly.

"Poor Christopher," she said, in an odd, crooning voice. "Poor, dear Christopher." And knowing that the exercise of one of these private, informal benefactions always placed him in an excellent humor, she wondered idly if it were not something of the sort which was responsible for his present good mood. . . .

Christopher traveled to Chicago by plane. Turning toward the South, he would take the rest of the tour by rail, for, although he was acutely conscious of the value of time, the communities in which he was most in demand were rarely served by the commercial airlines. On this tour he would visit briefly the states of Illinois, Indiana, Kentucky and Tennessee; his specific points of call were six cities of the type in which he enjoyed speaking most. They were small and entirely inconspicuous; having provided the country with no famous men, and possessing no crafts or industries of more than local importance, they were normally identified by their proximity to the nearest large city. The constant need for such identification had bred in the inhabitants of these small centers a curious sense of isolation, as well as a certain civic truculence; it was this fact which Christopher had grasped some years ago, and which he had turned to considerable advantage.

His first stop was New Paris, Indiana. He had not been there before, but he was not a stranger. As he pulled into the hideous stucco railroad station, he felt already the touch of the familiar; as he drove down the main street, past the pigeon-soiled statue of William Henry Harrison, he felt that he had come home. He had been fortunate enough to arrive on an afternoon of festival; the city, now a center for the production of inexpensive dentures, was deep in the remembrance of its agricultural past. On the old fairgrounds there was a fete: Christopher, whisked there by proud hosts, saw corn shuckers in their competitive fury; saw a cow being manually milked by a dedicated 4-H Club boy; saw a nimble old man, wild of eye, playing "Old Zip Coon" and "The Devil's Dream" on a battered fiddle. It was all real, heart-warming, good; it was only after he had been there for some time that he began to feel slightly impatient: remarkable as the performance was, there was no denying that it permitted little instructive conversation. On the whole, he was pleased rather than otherwise when he was taken to the welcoming tea, where gradually the proper balances were restored. Here there was good talk, for the municipal dignitaries who had assembled to meet Christopher were—apart from a certain aggressive insistence on the advanced state of their own community—attentive listeners. Christopher met the mayor: a tall, gaunt man with a Masonic key and a quick, spurting smile which revealed some debt to local industry. He presented Christopher with a huge metal zinnia; it was, he explained, an enduring replica of the official flower of the Hoosier state.

"From one of the country's most up-and-coming cities," he said, smiling swiftly, "to one of the country's most up-and-coming citizens. And now, Mr. Usher, may I ask: just what is your considered opinion of General George Catlett Marshall?"

From that point on, it was a splendid afternoon. . . .

At night, after the broadcast, there was the public lecture. For this had been reserved the auditorium of the Homer Capehart Memorial High School; long before the appointed hour, cars had begun to arrive from outlying hamlets and farms, for, no matter how up-and-coming the city, Christopher's audiences were seldom dominantly urban. In the auditorium, sections had been set apart for those prominent in politics, in fraternal work, in educational endeavor—even Dr. Mason Calcutt, venerable president of the Calcutt College of Chiropractic had promised to make one of his rare, nonacademic appearances. Fifteen minutes before lecture time, Christopher was backstage, checking his notes in final and careful survey.

He was furious; there had been a blunder. Before he set out on his lecture tours, it was his secretary's duty to fill in a mimeographed information blank for each city to be visited:

1) Name of city; nickname
2) Name of mayor; nickname
3) Leading citizens; occupations of
4) Imp. histor. events
5) Shrines, monuments, natur. phenomena
6) Princ. industries
7) Princ. lodges, societies
8) Princ. relig. groups
9) Items local humor

He shook his head in irritation; there had been a serious error on the sheet for New Paris. Opposite "Princ. industries" his secretary had written: "CORN, HOGS." The reference was hopelessly outmoded; Christopher had seen enough of this sensitive community to realize that the agricultural must necessarily be assigned to the quaint, indulgently remembered past. Still, exactly how to amend the mistake? He could not bring himself to write in "DENTURES" or "FALSE TEETH"; the blunt words, lacked style, dignity. Unquestionably there was some local euphemism with which he was unfamiliar. . . . Sighing, he decided to take the quick way out. He scratched out "CORN, HOGS" and substituted "IDEAS." It was unspecific but reliable; he had found that the communities in which he spoke were rarely distressed at the imputation to them of ceaseless mental activity. Sighing again, and jotting down a memorandum to take his secretary to task, he gathered his material together and prepared to go onstage.

He walked on with the mayor; applause broke out from all sides. Christopher saw at a glance that the setting was up to the anticipated standard; every seat occupied, every face eager, a multitude thirsting for knowledge. His feeling of annoyance vanished before this best of all medicines; now, at the center of the stage, he stood at attention, for he knew the unvarying routine to come. The houselights were extinguished; all applause died. Out of the darkness came the beam of a spotlight, focusing full upon a large American flag at the right corner of the stage; an electric fan, concealed behind the flag, started to whir, causing the flag to ripple fervently in the synthetic breeze. Coincidentally, a recording of the national anthem was played over the public-address system; Christopher and the mayor led the audience in strong song. This over, there was a momentary hush; Christopher felt a powerful surge of emotional strength, of pride. As often as he had been through this ceremony, the knowledge that it was all for God, for country, and for him never failed to leave him slightly breathless.

At the rostrum, the mayor had begun the speech of presentation. Judged even by the liberal standards of this part of the world, the introduction was a long one; it was, however, most generous, for the mayor spoke of Christopher with very nearly the same intensity of feeling with which he spoke of New Paris. At last came climactic words, Christopher rose and bowed slightly, there was a torrent of acclaim, and he began to talk.

A seasoned campaigner, he opened slowly, informally. His words— ". . . long admired the administrative abilities of my good friend, Mayor Ev Mosper . . . delightful meeting with the renowned educator and goodly healer, Dr. Mason Calcutt . . . revelation to stand quietly beneath the magnificent bronze statue of the Hero of Tippecanoe, the Ninth President of these United States . . . greatest of pleasures to visit a city so vitally concerned with the production of Ideas . . . community from which springs so much of the strength of our YMCA . . . legionnaires every-

where look with envy upon your Casper Stanwell Post
. . . source of deep regret that time does not permit a
thorough exploration of the wonders of the world-famed
Wabash Scenic Caverns . . ."—were received with the
expected mixture of astonishment and joy; they were delivered in tones appropriate to friendly discourse between
equals. It was not until he reached the body of his lecture
that he assumed the broadcast manner. From somewhere
in the audience came a gasp of recognition; then silence.
The lecture was under way.

In cities such as New Paris, Christopher gave, whenever
possible, his talk titled "One World and Your World";
it was this which he delivered tonight. A rousing philippic,
proof against the most apathetic listener, it was by all odds
the most successful of his many lectures. If it lacked
something of the spiritual ginger to be found in "Gandhi
and Christ," it more than made up for this in its greater
plasticity. Infinitely adaptable, it could be and was molded
to any set of local circumstances. Briefly, it revealed the
world in its simplest terms, as nothing more than a vast,
imperfect analogue of the community in which Christopher happened to be speaking. Tonight, two social
organisms—the world and New Paris—were placed side
by side; in the comparison, the world came off rather
badly. On the one hand there was disorder, poverty, im-
piety a polyglot chaos; on the other, there was neatness,
abundance, faith, a resolved monolingual blend. On the
one hand was the way of Ev Mosper, the Casper Stanwell

Post, the Hero of Tippecanoe; on the other, the way of Stalin, Mao, the State Department, the crafty British, the venal French. Where the world had failed, New Paris had come through. . . .

". . . and the reason is simple. The reason is there, *here*, for everyone to see. No mystery cloaks it; nothing is concealed from view. It's simply the story of a people who *pull together*, people of every race, color and creed, their heads held high, determined from the bottom of their stout hearts to make their city *work*, to make their city *live*. Yes, it's a lesson, a great lesson, one of the greatest in all history. Yet try to give that lesson to the world! Try to give that lesson to the so-called civilized nations of Europe! Try to give that lesson to those cynical statesmen, those leaders to whom double-talk and deceit come as natural as breathing, those same men to whose almighty wisdom the unhappy land of China can today bear mute testimony. . . ."

He went on, caught in the exhilarating rhythm of his own delivery, building step by step to the sanguine, the inspirational, the inevitable close. Could there, *would* there, one day be One World? YES—but only when those in high places were willing to abandon greed, pride, and self-interest, and come to the problems of the world with the one, simple, eminently workable approach: the approach that had been found, long years ago, in the city of New Paris!

There was deafening applause; there were whistles,

cheers, the stamping of feet; the Homer Capehart Memorial High School quivered with approval. Christopher stood, silent, smiling; he glanced covertly at his watch. The over-all delivery time of this talk was fifty-three minutes; tonight, thanks to the unprecedented frequency of the applause, it ran to a bit better than one hour and eight minutes. Never before had "One World and Your World" been so flatteringly protracted; Christopher waved happily at the crowd and the applause grew louder. It was undoubtedly one of the most successful talks of a not unsuccessful career, and as he stood on the stage, bending graciously to meet the glorious gales of acclaim, he could not help but regard it as an omen. It all tied in, he thought: the victory over Udolpho, the new life to come, a long string of nights just such as this, stretching away in infinite procession into the golden future. He had never before, he decided, been so completely, so unreservedly, happy. . . .

This performance was repeated, with minor variations, in each of the remaining cities of the tour. He gave "One World and Your World" everywhere save in St. Paul, Tennessee; there he had given it only the year before. St. Paul, therefore, got "Gandhi"; the results were perhaps a shade less spectacular, but quite good enough.

Yet important and satisfying as was his work on the lecture platform, Christopher did not forget the primacy of his nightly broadcasts to the nation; before he had left on tour, he had arranged to originate these broadcasts each night from the station of the radio network most convenient to the city in which he visited. As the radio network was a large one, with a great many stations, this posed no problem; on two occasions, indeed, Christopher was able to broadcast directly from the hall where he was to lecture, thus providing his lecture audience a double joy. The preparation of the broadcasts on the road was not perceptibly more difficult than at home; while he was necessarily denied such ready access to his usual news sources, he had the immense advantage of knowing his own mind, of knowing precisely what he wished to tell the world, regardless of any sudden turn in the news. Thus, the deprivation was of small consequence. A quick look at the latest developments on the nearest press association wire, the rapid ingestion of those items which seemed of some importance, a brief session at the typewriter, and then, alchemically produced, another broadcast was ready for immediate delivery to a waiting public. . . .

In various quarters, among various of Christopher's friends and associates, these broadcasts were variously received. . . .

Adam Flair listened. At home, in bed, he listened with closed eyes as Christopher urged the country on to inspired impracticalities in the interest of coolie emancipation. Adam had been listening to the radio for more than an hour; he looked older. He had heard the usual ghastly mélange of relentless humor, popular songs and gossip; he considered not so much the quality of the entertainment—he was long past that—as the quality of the entertainers. He knew them all; every one was his co-worker in one of the largest and most substantial of American industries. Of these people who joined him in his diurnal labors, Adam had his opinion, and when he was alone, he voiced it often.

"Fools," he said thoughtfully. "The whole business is the imbeciles' New Jerusalem. . . ."

Now, he listened to Christopher Usher. Of Christopher, the most important of these co-workers, he had a somewhat different opinion. This too, under similar conditions, he voiced often, and as he listened now to the celebrated tones in their resonant progression, he voiced it again.

"Without a doubt," he said slowly, "the premier bastard of this our noble land. . . ."

Mr. Churchill Chan listened. In the company of two other Chinese, he sat in an elaborately furnished room in the nation's capital. The three listened in silence; from time to time two of them turned and focused upon Mr. Chan long stares of Oriental disbelief. Mr. Chan shrugged slightly; his eyebrows rose, not much, but enough to lend the smooth old face an expression of eloquent distress.

"A man of great good heart, perhaps," he sighed. "It is all quite hopeless . . . I will try again . . . and again. . . ."

One of the other Chinese frowned perplexedly. "He is a man of influence?" he asked. "*This* man?"

"Yes, yes, of great influence . . . it is a most strange country."

The other Chinese shrugged his acceptance of an irrelevant fact. "He understands nothing. You must tell him."

"Tell him," echoed Mr. Churchill Chan. He smiled sadly. "Ah yes," he said, "that is precisely what is most difficult . . . *most* difficult. . . ."

In a baroque mansion in Chicago, Mr. Bernie Udolpho listened while parading up and down in his library. This was a large and bookless room, voluptuously appointed in the style of the Ottoman Empire; across the ankle deep carpets Mr. Bernie prowled, clad in a bath towel. He seldom wore clothing in his own home: it was here that he had to think, to make the big decisions while indulging in a perpetual round of baths and unguent applications. As the broadcast progressed, he continued to walk about the room: a little, round, beige figure, glistening with the oil of Spanish walnuts.

"I dunno," he said aloud; fat little fingers beat in meditative tattoo upon a spongy lower lip. "I dunno, I dunno. . . ."

In Christopher's home, both Meredith and the general listened. Meredith listened in silence; the general lent Christopher enthusiastic vocal support. The old warrior's overnight stay had now, at the end of a week, given promise of even further extension; he had somehow received crisp orders from Washington, and each morning, humming blithely, he was called for in a staff car and driven off to his new duties. These were agreeable enough and not unduly taxing: they consisted of visits to the different high schools of the city where, under the wild misapprehension that the youths seated sullenly before him aspired to immediate enlistment, he spoke in glowing terms of the military life. This was old stuff to the general; few knew better than he how to coax the potential recruit into camp:

". . . up before dawn on a cold winter's morning, boys!" he would cry rhapsodically. "Up and out into the nippy air for a long 'tone-up' run before breakfast. . . ."

He passed on to them, freely, the little tips to success, the short cuts to leadership, the knowledge which could only be acquired after a lifetime of professional service:

". . . take plenty of cold baths, boys! A good soldier is a clean soldier; a clean soldier is a good soldier! And remember your feet! One of the great secrets of being a good soldier is to have healthy feet. Never wear the same pair of shoes two days in a row. I never have, and the result is, boys, that today I have grand feet. . . ."

He taught them the techniques for defense and survival in an atomic age:

"How many of you young lads know how to stalk an enemy Indian-style? Put up your hands. . . ."

All in all, apart from infrequent periods of depression, periods as transient as a wink, the general was supremely satisfied with his lot. Now, as Christopher sounded the notes of vigorous conclusion, the general positively chortled in unqualified approval.

"Bravo!" he cried, turning to Meredith. "Straight from the shoulder, my dear! The whole truth and nothing but the truth; how rarely it is heard today! I swear this husband of yours gets better by the minute. There are times, my dear," he confided, more solemnly, "when I am quite certain that he comes very close to being the *voice* of our *national conscience!*"

"I'm not at all sure Christopher would disagree with that," Meredith said, smiling at the general. Somewhat to her astonishment, a week of almost uninterrupted association with this fantastic old man had altered her opinion of him for the better; there were moments when her feeling toward him was one of affection. He seldom bothered her; although he talked unwearyingly of himself and his world, as Christopher's wife she had grown to accept the absence of reticence in others as an established condition of her existence. For the most part she did not hear him, for she was an adept at the art of social insulation; yet on those occasions when she did listen, she found his courtly recitation of the imagined glories of the past sometimes amusing, sometimes not a little sad. She came to think of him as a quaint and touching survival of an age that never was, a relic at once benign, jaunty and unreal, and she said to him now, "Actually, General, I don't think Christopher would disagree with you on many counts. He's been in wonderful spirits recently; I think very probably your visit is the reason."

"And very probably, my dear," said the general, "it is *not*." He smiled mysteriously. "No, no, no. You flatter me, my dear, but I hardly think that the presence of an old soldier is the cause of such well-being. No, I think that for that you must look elsewhere."

"Oh?" In the arch old voice there had been more than a hint of the possession of special information; puzzled, Meredith asked: "And where would you suggest that I look, General? Have you any specific ideas?"

An elegant hand fluttered in protest. "I never violate a confidence, my dear," he said gaily. "Always supposing, of course, that there *was* a confidence to begin with. You haven't heard anything from Christopher, then?"

"No. Not about anything particularly important, that is. Should I have?"

"No, no, not at all. Perhaps you had better forget that I have said anything, my dear." He twinkled at her; then, surprisingly he began to sing in a playful voice; hastily improvising primitive lyrics, he applied them to a tune of the nursery.

"Surprises are the best," the old man sang. "Surprises are the best; heigh ho the derry-oh, surprises are the best. . . ."

Further song was prevented by the unexpected entrance of Dr. Wrenn.

"I thought I heard music," he said, kissing his daughter.

"A masculine voice." He stared at the general with polite incredulity. "You were not singing, General, surely?"

"Nothing of consequence, nothing at all," the general said hastily. He was not a man of great intelligence, but in common with old campaigners everywhere, he had an instinct for self-preservation. Few knew better than he the importance to one's career of the martial aspect, the good form, perpetually worn; few were more aware that to be suspected of frivolity by important civilians was to invite oblivion. "A note or two, no more," he said, the fruity tones disclaiming irresponsibility. "Actually, Doctor, our evening has been to most serious purpose; it has been most interesting. I have been explaining to your daughter something of the hardship of desert warfare; and then, most recently, we have just finished listening to Christopher's broadcast. It was excellent: I do not think I exaggerate when I say that we were held absolutely spellbound!"

"I have never ceased to be astonished," observed the doctor, "by the great numbers of adults in this country who appear to be devoted to sports. I did not know that you were among them, General."

"Sports . . . ?"

"And yet I presume it is a concomitant of the military life, the necessary relaxation after the rigors of the field. One spends the long day in battle; in the evening, one seeks surcease in the nepenthe of softball, or clock golf. It is a healthy balance; speaking as a physician, General, I think you are wise to maintain it."

97

"Ah," said the general, with the wise nod with which he was accustomed to conceal total incomprehension. Aware that not everyone of his age enjoyed his own robust health, he wondered if this baffling contemporary were not perhaps hard of hearing. "A sporting program has its place indeed in army life, Doctor!" he shouted, and was slightly disconcerted to note that the doctor winced in all-too-evident reproach of the heightened tones. He continued more softly: "I wonder if there has not been a slight misunderstanding? I have been listening to Christopher, your son-in-law. . . ."

"You could do no better," said the doctor courteously. "Of all the men I know, he is the most intimately acquainted with the minutiae of athletics. It may seem an inconsequential accomplishment for a fully grown male, but then we live in an age of specialization, eh, General?"

"Ah," said the general, nodding even more wisely. "Yes, yes indeed. How right you are!" Suddenly wary, he suspected deviousness: it was in this language of the partially unbalanced that traps were sometimes laid. He rose quickly and said, "Well, off to work, to prepare for another day's labor in the vineyards. I sometimes think an old soldier's work is never done. You'll excuse me, I know."

Dr. Wrenn watched him go and said, "What a comfort to know that our country's defenses are in capable hands. There are times when I am seriously worried about the possibility of war; then I think of the general, and my fears become quiet."

"You leave the general alone," Meredith said. "I want to talk to you about Christopher." She began another battle in the long campaign; tonight she stressed the extended parade of good deeds, of private charities unsung and unacknowledged. The doctor listened, profoundly unimpressed.

"Nothing could interest me less," he said finally, "than this litany of Christopher's philanthropies. You do not persuade me, my dear: I will not cuddle up to this husband of yours simply because he provides a turkey dinner for a widow at Christmas. Come now, let us talk of something more congenial, and do not," he warned, lifting up his hand, "*kindly* do not tell me what Christopher told the world tonight. That I really think I could not bear. . . ."

In the tasteful modernity of her hotel suite Lura crouched by the radio, listening intently—but unfortunately, not to Christopher. It was rank disloyalty, but she could not help herself. Once a week, there was a directly competitive broadcast which summoned her like a call to arms; once a week, Mabel Prune was on the air with her Hollywood Bulletin Board. Lura, fascinated, listened as out of the West came the familiar oleaginous cackle of authority, streaming forth its message of saccharin and spite. . . .

". . . Judy Surprise, the lovely Paramount starlet, and Ringo Mazzucelli, my *favorite* agent, have discovered each other and are in *love*; Ringo has turned playwright for the occasion and has written a *play* for Judy which my spies tell me is the *best* story since Walter Hugo, the well-known French writer . . . *poor* Nancy Featherfeet! A permanent wave machine in one of our *best-known* hair-dressing parlors went out of control the other day and burnt Nancy's *wonderful* auburn hair so badly that she is now completely *bald!* This is a *terrible* blow to her fiance, Mike Broom, whose divorce from Esther Dawn becomes final the first of next week . . . Rory McManus was arrested *again* this week on a charge of disturbing the *peace*. Some of us tried to warn Rory *just* after he deserted his lovely young wife and their *three little children,* but he just *wouldn't* listen . . . petite Mimi Penseroso, Hal Bimbaum's *latest* foreign discovery, after only *one week* in the United States said that her *favorite* dish in all the *world* was the *hot dog!* Good for you, Mimi, that's the American way . . . biggest surprise of the week was Bubbles de Vries's announcement that she will enter a *convent* in Iceland as soon as she finishes *Strip-Tease* for M-G-M. . . ."

Once, four years ago, Lura had been the subject of brief, unflattering mention by Mabel; though similar good fortune was unlikely now, she listened eagerly, an exile in a distant land, the cackling voice the sole thread of connection with her spiritual home. She listened for names: names of streets, restaurants, rivals, chums, ex-husbands; hungrily, she devoured the scraps from Mabel's table. Despite Christopher's attentions, there were intervals when Lura missed the good times, the excitements, the profane joys of the golden land she had abandoned. At such moments, she sighed, a homesick little girl; not even the thought of Christopher, but an inch away on the radio dial, was of much help in such an abyss of despair. . . .

five

HOMEWARD BOUND, CHRISTOPHER STOPPED OVERNIGHT IN Washington. He did so with reluctance, for of all the cities he visited, either through choice or vocational compulsion, Washington was the one he liked least. He avoided it whenever possible; it was here, he thought, in this raucous community, that the art of conversation had died, choking to death on a surfeit of words. From bitter experience, he knew that here the listener was unknown; everyone was a talker. From staid old barbers down to freshman senators, all talked with the air of immeasurable authority which comes to those who dwell close to the horse's mouth. For such importunate amateurs, Christopher could not help but feel the natural contempt of the professional; all the same, he found their society decidedly disquieting, and it was only under conditions of extreme urgency that he grudgingly endured it.

Tonight, the affair was something of a "must": it was a party given by the musical comedy songstress who had, within the week, been appointed ambassador to Turkey. Quite by chance, the social week in Washington had been a dull one; this contributed to the success of the new ambassador's party. It had taken on the necessary proportions of a state affair: ministers, envoys, departmental secretaries came in abundance, looking discreet, secure in the knowledge that as invited guests they ranked in importance only below the gossip columnists. Even the White House had taken notice: a presidential aide, in the uniform of his country's service, lent the affair the dignity of his office by jabbing at the ladies with an electric cane. Over in a corner, two members of the Soviet Secretariat were surreptitiously stuffing their pockets with cubes of sugar; in the center of the room the ambassador herself was singing a *double-entendre* song. It was a superb gathering, quite the best of the young season, and Christopher's heart sank as, entering, he saw the throng of adept monologuists.

A pale bald man with a great curving prow of a nose came speeding toward him; he was a rival broadcaster for whom Christopher cherished a particular dislike.

"Hello, Usher, down from the woods for our little shebang, eh? Good, good. Everyone should visit the nerve center, so to speak, every once in a while. Helps one keep in touch with what's going on." He looked around him discontentedly. "Of course for me it's no treat. Perfectly dreadful, as a matter of fact. I go to so many of these things I get sick of them all. Still, in all conscience, I have to; there's always my responsibility to my listeners. Well, well, well. What do you think of this mess in China, anyway?"

It was a calculated insult; the man, as everyone else, knew precisely what Christopher thought of the Chinese situation. Stiffly, Christopher said: "It's fairly obvious, I should think. There's only one honorable course of action, once you acknowledge the existence of any moral responsibility on our part—"

"I'll tell you what I think," said the pale man, who, in accordance with the little courtesies of his profession, had been waving at someone across the room while Christopher talked. "I'll tell you exactly what I think. I'll give you, Usher, the results of a thirty-three years' study of that country and its people. I say it's a bad business, that it's time we learned to face facts, that it's time we wrote China off the books as just another bad debt. And I don't say that, mind you, simply because I'm disappointed in Chiang. Chiang did let me down, but fundamentally it's a question of practical policy. Look at it this way, Usher, and I think you'll see the whole picture in a clearer perspective. One, we need—"

"Excuse me," Christopher said, backing away hastily.

"Another time; I see someone I absolutely must talk to. Excuse me, please." He moved off rapidly, in rare retreat. At another time, in another place, he would have responded to the challenge; now, here, somehow the desire for battle had been drained from him. Voices rose on every side, a confusion of unrelated languages and themes; Christopher, unilingual and unhappy, slid past a group speaking in a strange tongue that sounded like gargling, and came up abruptly against the Reverend Dr. Barclay Gruel.

"My dear Usher!" exclaimed Dr. Gruel, in obvious delight. "What an unexpected pleasure!" He was a beaming, sportily-clad little clergyman who was much in vogue at the moment; his popularity was ascribable both to his mellow voice and his utter absence of any positive religious convictions. "No dogmas for me," he was fond of proclaiming, his eyes twinkling tolerance. "To each his own, in the phrase of the day." He preached often, but because he was so eager to avoid any conceivable offense to anyone, his sermons were never concerned with human behavior; rather, he guided his flock to the Creator (if, indeed, One there was) by elaborate homilies based upon the relatively safe world of the brute and the inanimate. He spoke on "The Bruised Rose," "Wheat and Chaff," "The Wiser Horse," "A Descending Redwood," "White Cliffs of Dover"; now an established preacher, he gazed without rancor or envy upon his more secular fellow.

"Enlighten a poor parson upon the state of the world at large, my dear Usher. Do you think that there really might be another war? For my part, I sincerely hope not. The havoc, the waste, the destruction . . . by the bye, how long will you stay in our fair city?"

"Only overnight, I'm afraid. I—"

"What a pity!" sighed the doctor. "What a great pity. I must confess I had hoped to see you among those present at our little service on Sunday morning."

"I should be delighted, but unfortunately—"

"We are quite crowded these days. I attribute it to the needs of the times rather than to my own poor skill as a preacher. Still, on Sunday I shall say a few words on a subject which you might find of great interest. It will be, I think, rather controversial; how delighted I would have been to gain your reaction. One in my position of comparative insularity depends so much upon the considered judgment of the observant laity."

"That's very kind of you, Doctor. As I say, I only wish it were possible—"

"I shall speak," said the man of God, "upon soil erosion. Have you read *Our Plundered Planet*? It gives one pause to think, my dear Usher. I am attacking it from a somewhat different approach; it is a theme," he said, his mellow voice rolling out, "upon which I may be forced to speak rather *bluntly*. . . ."

The voice flowed on, speaking with some passion of alluvial deposits, watersheds, irrigation and cloudbursts; before this pulpit preview, the desire for consultation with Christopher on world affairs seemed to have been forgotten. It was some minutes before Christopher could free himself; when he did so, it was with a sense of despair, an awareness that nowhere in this noisy room was there an island of escape. Fretfully, he felt more keenly than ever the absence of a wholesome leavening of Little People. Wandering about, he heard the musical comedy star who, having finished her song, was now discussing her qualifications for her new role.

". . . so I said to him 'Hold it, sugar, hold it! So I know nothing from Turkey. So Turkey knows nothing from me, so we start off even!' So I got the job. But I'm learning. I'm learning fast. Up to last week, all I knew about Turkey was how to spell Constantinople—you sing it: C-O-N-S-T-A-N-T-I-N-O-P-L-E; did you ever play that game?—and eat shish-kebab. But I'm coming along; don't worry about little Betty. She can take care of herself and the U.S.A. I want you all to come and see me once I get set . . . say, do you think I'll have to wear one of those funny little red hats? Hah?"

"Fez," said the pale broadcaster with the big nose. "It's called a fez. Listen, Betty, you must let me tell you about Kemal Ataturk before you go. It's impossible to understand modern Turkey without understanding Kemal . . ."

"Kemal Shemmel!" cried the ambassador, with a howl of laughter. "Come on, boys, who'd like another song . . . ?"

Not even this prime instance of administrative folly, here before his eyes and fodder for a dozen broadcasts, could excite him, and as the brassy contralto of the new ambassador rang out with the assurance that heaven above had made her for love, he hurried away, glumly computing the number of minutes yet remaining before he might take his leave. These occasions, he knew, were governed by an inelastic protocol; one had to be there, to be seen, to greet one or two in authority before effecting the welcome departure. . . .

"Christopher. Heard you were here. Been looking all over for you. Everywhere."

At the ominous words, Christopher turned swiftly, expecting the worst: another broadcaster, a sponger, the British ambassador. To his intense relief, it was only Leonard Keisler.

"Ah, Leonard," he said. "It's good to see you." It was not, at the moment, an overstatement. Keisler was an advertising man, a lean, morose figure whom Christopher remembered as possessing the positive virtue of an almost preternatural taciturnity. Indeed, throughout the not unassertive fraternity to which he belonged there ran the derisive slogan: "Keisler Is Quiet." Recalling this now with pleasure, Christopher said again, "Good to see you, Leonard. And how is everything in your part of the world? Doing as well as usual, I hope?"

"Mm," said Keisler. The vast network of melancholy lines became even more sharply defined on the solemn, ovoid face. "Look, Christopher," he said. "Came over to tell you how sorry I was. Terribly sorry. Whole thing's awful. Damn shame."

"Awful? Shame?" For Keisler, this was volubility; Christopher frowned his incomprehension. "I'm afraid I don't quite understand, Leonard."

Keisler nodded sadly, wisely; it was the nod of one who knew and who sympathized. "Only heard yesterday," he said, rather apologetically. "Been away. Called you up, no answer. Glad to run into you here. Wanted to say sorry. Damned sorry. Anything I can do . . ."

Quite suddenly, Christopher realized that *he* was the object of commiseration. But why? For what reason? Alarmingly, it occurred to him that these mournful tones were appropriate to domestic catastrophe: a sickness, even a *death* . . . the names of those nearest and dearest to him flashed across his mind. In this moment of crisis, he was no longer the commentator, he was the family man: he thought of Lura, his wife. "What is it, Keisler?" he said sharply. "Who's ill?"

"Ill? Someone ill? I don't know."

Relieved, Christopher said, "It's simply that I thought from the way you talked . . . what are you talking about, anyway?"

"Udolpho," Keisler said simply.

"*Udolpho?*"

Keisler nodded again. "Damn fool. Shortsighted. Biggest men sometimes make worst mistakes. No need to

feel badly. You did great job for him. Should have re-
newed. Old saying: penny-wise, pound-foolish."

To this condensed and cryptic speech, Christopher
listened, at first baffled, and then with a mounting amaze-
ment as gradually the puzzle took shape, and he realized
what the man was actually saying.

"Wait one minute," he said abruptly. "Wait just one
minute, Leonard. I want to get this straight. Are you trying to tell me that Udolpho isn't going to renew my contract? Is that what you're saying?"

"Mm. Heard only yesterday. Excellent source. Ollie
Maypole. Ollie's on inside. Damn shame, Christopher."

Christopher smiled. "Listen, Leonard," he said. "Listen
to me. I appreciate your sympathy, but believe me, it's
completely uncalled for. You're way off base on this:
Udolpho is renewing and renewing quickly. Let me set
you right on this." With a minimum of deletion, and with
perhaps his own part slightly magnified by memory, he
told the story of his victorious negotiations in Adam
Flair's office. "This is for your ears alone, Leonard," he
cautioned, concluding. "I'm telling this to you simply so
you can see the whole matter in the proper perspective,
so that you can see that Christopher Usher isn't ready
for the rubbish pile just yet." He smiled again at this.

Keisler's melancholy face regarded him doubtfully.
"Good news," he said, with just the barest touch of disappointment edging his words. "Didn't know that. Still,
got my information from best source. Ollie Maypole. Not

often wrong." His mouth slightly open, he stood in dyspeptic appreciation of the good tidings; then, grasping at a straw, he asked: "Udolpho actually *sign?*"

"If you mean did he put his name to a contract then and there, the answer is no . . ."

"Ah," said Keisler, with a little nod of satisfaction.

". . . but that's hardly the point; that's purely a matter of form. The point is that from the atmosphere of the negotiations, from his attitude, you could tell that it was just as good as signed, sealed and delivered. It was unmistakable, Leonard."

"Mm," said Keisler, more cheerfully. "No signature? Well." He began to move away, his work accomplished. "Got to go," he said. "Appointment. Hope you're right, Christopher. Ought to know. Still, my information. Ollie Maypole. On the inside. Way inside. Better check up. Funny things happen. So long. See you."

"No need to check up," Christopher called after him. "Although you might check up, Leonard. You might check up on your friend Maypole. And when you do, tell him for me that he'd better get *further* inside!" He felt immeasurably bucked up by the whole conversation, with its climax of witty farewell; the whole thing had been one in the eye for Keisler as well as for the mysterious Maypole. In such good humor did the encounter place him that for some few minutes, before finally leaving, he wandered about from group to group, saying nothing, but listening, half-hearing, even, as (a) a Soviet attaché explained in some detail the discovery of the North American continent by the Russian explorer, Columbus; (b) a senator from Idaho discussed the national economy from the point of view of the Big Potato; (c) a correspondent of a well-known liberal magazine was revealing, with great fluency, that the present excessive tides along the coast of Sweden were directly attributable to the wily Vatican. . . .

It was only that night, as he lay in his hotel bed, just before going to sleep, that the words of Leonard Keisler returned to him, this time with a force all out of proportion to their value. There was no truth in them, of course, not a bit; yet the very fact that it was Keisler who had uttered them was faintly troubling, for Christopher had suddenly remembered something else about this long, sepulchral man. In addition to his fabled reticence, he had in the trade the somewhat enviable reputation of being "in on the death." Like some solemn carrion, Keisler could sniff out the potential decay, the approach of the knife; to a hundred men, happy in their work, assured of their futures, Keisler had one day appeared, first harbinger of ruin. It was in tribute to the melancholy powers of this gifted man that Christopher, for all his confidence, twisted uneasily in the final seconds of his wakefulness, and reflected that he had not, after all, heard from Udolpho since the conference, that this was of no importance whatsoever, but that on the strength of Keisler's reputation alone many a man less secure than himself might well have made an anxious telephone call, seeking information, reassurance. . . .

He made the call the following morning. He flew back from Washington, and before going to his home, before, even, contacting Lura, he taxied from the airport to his office where, after a quick and unrewarding survey of the messages on his desk, he placed the call to Chicago. He was put through to Mr. Udolpho immediately; in its uninflected detachment, the little industrialist's voice was calm, clear and somehow discouraging.

"Yeh?"

"Good morning, Mr. Udolpho," Christopher said heartily. "This is Christopher Usher."

"Yeh. I know."

"How are you?" Thinking that perhaps the light touch was called for, Christopher said, "Are you gradually becoming accustomed to civilization after your travels through darkest Europe?"

"Yeh, yeh."

There was no doubt about it: the amenities were not easily observed with this strange man; more briskly, Christopher said: "I'll tell you why I called, Mr. Udolpho. I hadn't heard from you regarding our little talk of a week or so ago, and since I've been on the road, so to speak, and not too easily contacted, I've been wondering if by any chance you've arrived at a final decision."

He thought he heard a hoarse, chuckling sound. "Yeh?" said Mr. Udolpho.

"I mean, of course," Christopher said hastily, "that if you have arrived at any such decision, I'd appreciate knowing it as soon as possible—"

"You nervous?"

"No, no, certainly not. There's nothing to be nervous about. It's simply that—"

"You in a hurry? A big rush?" The questions were not truculent; they conveyed, rather, a sense of gentle amusement which Christopher found disconcerting.

"No hurry at all," he said quickly. "The matter is entirely in your hands, of course, and can be decided at your convenience. Naturally, however, there are certain plans and arrangements I'd like to make as soon as I could—"

"Yeh, yeh," said Mr. Udolpho. "Well, I tell you what. I dunno yet. I'm pretty busy now. I'll let you know in a week."

"I see. Well then, I'll expect to hear something definite from you within the week—"

"*In* a week," corrected Mr. Udolpho. "One week from today I'll let you know. You got anything else on your mind?"

"No, nothing in particular. I know how busy you are at this time of year, so I'll just say good-by and—"

"Good-by," said Mr. Udolpho; Christopher heard the faint terminal click. He sat for a moment, staring at the telephone; the talk had been far from satisfactory. Although, basically, nothing seemed to have changed, it was precisely this fact which troubled Christopher. An undecided, noncommittal Udolpho ten days ago was one thing—then, in the almost electric radiance cast by Christopher's on-the-spot apologia, it had seemed that eventually he could turn but one way; now, a week and a half removed from the moment of eloquence, the development seemed less inevitable. For the first time, Christopher saw in Udolpho's prolonged indecision a drastic potential. It worried him. He frowned, rose, and stared at himself in the mirror. Sometimes, plagued by the varying afflictions to which the prominent fall heir, he found great comfort in the steady contemplation of his own strong features. This morning, the procedure did not work; turning in irritation from the mirror, he plunged into the reliable consolations of his accumulated mail. It was wonderful mail, inspiring mail, each long letter an unquestioning endorsement of Usher the Voice and Usher the Man; yet this morning it was all somehow ineffective. Across each page there seemed to float the grim, prophetic specter of Leonard Keisler, followed by the echo of a hoarse and heartless chuckle. To Christopher, it was all thoroughly disturbing. . . .

Later that day, he went to see Adam Flair.

"Come in, Christopher." Adam was in a mood of rare geniality; only that morning he had attended the obsequies for the elderly actor who for years, and despite the ailments of advanced age, had played the role of Sonny Muscle, juvenile hero of a thousand broadcast adventures. For some time Adam had been dissatisfied with the old man's performance, yet a sense of loyalty plus an awareness of inevitable union reprisals prevented dismissal. But now he had died, mercifully at the end of a chapter; for the continuance of the series, a new Sonny Muscle would have to be found. In his pleasure over this just if unexpected stroke of fate, Adam spoke reminiscently and with a certain fondness of the old actor.

"In a way, Christopher, he was as dedicated to his art as any man I ever knew. His natural voice, you knew, had a tendency toward the whisky baritone; hardly the voice for Sonny Muscle. The old man went to a surgeon; the result was that horrid teen-age squawk that stayed with him to the moment of his death. And he lived his role up to the hilt every minute of the day; as he became more senile, his identity became more deeply submerged in the personality of Sonny. In his last years he rarely talked of anything other than weenie roasts, juke boxes and hot rods. I won't pretend, of course, that he didn't present a certain problem to management. He was a dreadful ham, and as he grew increasingly wrinkled and emaciated, he was obsessed with the idea that he should make personal appearances. Naturally, as our one desire was to keep him concealed from public view at all times, we had to exercise some care. . . ."

"Yes, yes, I suppose so," Christopher said, rather abstractedly. He was not in the mood to listen to the merits of an actor, however dedicated, however recently deceased. "Listen, Adam," he said. "On my trip through the West, I've been doing a lot of thinking. Specifically, I've been thinking about Udolpho."

"Ah," said Adam, "I like to think about Udolpho, and frequently do so. It helps to keep me humble."

Christopher stared at him. "That's a peculiar reaction," he said. "He doesn't make me feel humble."

"We operate on diverse levels, Christopher. You've brought him to his knees, you see, and that makes all the difference."

It was, just possibly, irony; Christopher decided to pass it by. "What I'm getting at, Adam, is that I've been thinking of the entire matter in a different light. I think that it's about time I did. After all, it's been ten days since our meeting; have you heard from him at all?"

"Not a syllable. I might add, at this point, that I've never quite believed in that old saw about no news being good news. Considering your profession, I shouldn't think you would, either, but that's neither here nor there. What have you heard from him, by the way?"

"Nothing," said Christopher swiftly. He had a plan, a tentative solution, and in its interest he had decided not to mention the telephone conversation with Udolpho that morning. He began to pace back and forth across the office; like many another tactician, he found mobility to be an aid to exposition. "Actually," he said, "I know that Udolpho will come through. I knew it ten days ago and I know it now. But I don't like all this delay. I can appreciate the fact that he's a busy man, but so am I, and I think *he* should appreciate that. If he doesn't, he should be made to. So . . ."

"So," said Adam, "you've decided to make him. You're thinking of forcing the issue, of speeding things up a bit. Is that it, Christopher?"

"You might put it that way, yes." Anticipating opposition, he raised an admonishing hand. "Now wait, Adam. Hear me out. This is important, important to both of us. As I may have told you before, I think I understand Udolpho fairly well—"

"From time to time," Adam said, "you've mentioned it."

"—and if I tell you again it's only to point out that I understand exactly why he's acting this way now. It isn't that he's being malicious; it's simply that this is his way of doing business. He feels that he doesn't have to move in a hurry; he feels that it's to his advantage to put other people on tenterhooks, so to speak. He feels that he's in the driver's seat, that he can call the turn whenever and wherever he pleases. That's the psychology of the dictator, Adam; I've studied it for years."

"Yes, I know." It was not a busy afternoon, and Adam had no other appointments, but habit was strong with him, and now, as in all conferences with Christopher in the past, he glanced pointedly at his watch. "Dispensing for the moment with the question of your studies," he said, "and specifically and briefly, what's on your mind?"

"Boiled down to a few words, it comes to this: I think we should let him know he's not the only pebble on the beach." He watched Adam carefully, wondering about the success of the necessary deception. Obviously, he could not confess to Adam his present doubts; he could not admit that what he desired was not acceleration but certitude. The reply from Udolpho would arrive in a week; it was with a view toward molding that reply rather than hastening it that he sought to bring new pressures to bear, to apply the additional squeeze. For this, he would require Adam's co-operation.

"Actually, Adam, I think our course is fairly clear," he pursued. "I think that all we have to do is point out to him, unmistakably but not offensively, of course, that he is *not* alone in the driver's seat."

"That should surprise him," Adam said. He closed his eyes; the pleasant effects of the morning funeral were beginning to wear off. "Hints of competition, I suppose," he said. "You're suggesting that we tell Udolpho to hurry up and pick the peach or we'll let some other boys into the orchard?"

"Well, what's so wrong with that? Is it so improbable that several concerns might be eager to sponsor a top-ranking commentator?"

"I don't know; is it? Just for the record, you might name

some of these concerns that you have in mind. Name two. Name *one*."

Christopher threw up his hands, dismissing detail. "That's hardly my province, Adam. That's your job. Commercially speaking, my responsibility is to provide an audience who have enough confidence in me and what I stand for to make it worth while for a sponsor to advertise his products on my broadcast. I don't think I'm being boastful when I say that I've always fulfilled that responsibility. The records prove that my story is a success story. It's your responsibility to sell that success story to any new sponsor. And personally, Adam, I don't think you'd have the slightest trouble doing so."

"The tragic feature of conversations such as these," Adam said, "is that you really mean what you say." He looked speculatively at Christopher, then turned to stare out the window. "Other sponsors," he said thoughtfully. "Isn't that a new line for you, Christopher? It almost makes me wonder if I'm not witnessing a crumbling of self-confidence. You're sure you haven't communicated with Udolpho?"

"Naturally I'm sure!" He spoke more loudly, assumed indignation shoring up the false denial. "Look here, Adam, as soon as you've finished reading secondary meanings into everything I say, perhaps we can discuss this matter seriously. After all, it's something that affects both of us."

"Wrong," Adam said. "One hundred per cent wrong. It affects you, not me." He spun around in his chair;

behind the youthful face there had begun to throb the dull headache of one who was both middle-aged and harassed. "Let's cut out this diddling around, Christopher," he said abruptly. "Let's talk a little turkey. I'm not too busy this afternoon, but I'm too busy for this. First of all, get rid of this notion of forcing Udolpho. That's nonsense and you know it. Or at least I hope you do."

"Is it? You have a short memory, Adam. As I remember it, I did something of the sort about ten days ago and didn't come off too badly. You're a good fellow, Adam, but you hate to admit you've been wrong."

Adam groaned. "You did it ten days ago!" he echoed. "You remind me of the little boy who prodded the bear with the stick, Christopher. He got away with it the first time; it wasn't until the next time that he got his head clawed off. And right now you don't even know that you did get away with it the first time; he may be getting ready to rip you into bits. If I were you, Christopher, I'd let well enough alone and get down on my knees and say my prayers. And don't pray for a miracle; just stick to your daily bread."

Christopher smiled. "You're an alarmist, Adam. Besides, why all this concern over me? It seems to me that you ought to start thinking about yourself. It seems to me that the network has more than a slight stake in this, after all. Don't forget that if Udolpho *should* try any funny business, the network—*and* you, Adam—just might stand to lose as much and maybe more than I would."

"I've already told you," Adam said wearily, "that this affects you, not me." He stood up; he had made a decision; it was, once more, time for another of the frank employer-employee talks at which he was rather good, and which he never failed to enjoy. "Christopher," he said, "just for once, I want you to understand something. To make sure that you do, I'm going to talk to you as I should have long ago. Let's say I'm going to talk to you as a father."

Christopher smiled again; he could go along with a game. "Go right ahead, Father," he said. "Tell me all the facts of life."

"I intend to," said Adam. "First of all, I want you to get any idea of companionship in disaster out of your head. You stand or fall alone; remember that. I'd like to see you stand, if only for the fact that it means less trouble for everyone. But if you should go down, you go down by your lonesome; don't try to tug us with you. As far as we're concerned, you'll be all done. We'll still be on cordial terms with Udolpho. He'll still have advertising dollars to spend, and it's my business to see that he spends them with us. If not on you, then on someone else. You say you're a success story, Christopher; maybe you are. The point is that Udolpho will then be looking for another success story, and you can believe this or not, but we'll have a hatful to show him. You'd be astonished at how many success stories I can drag up when there's an extra dollar at stake. No, Christopher, if you go there'll be no moaning at the bar; I'll sell someone else to little Bernie before you're out of the building. It's a humiliating thing to learn, Christopher, but the fact of the matter is that you are among the replaceables!"

Christopher stared at him incredulously; in the last few seconds, the bare little office had acquired an atmosphere of betrayal, double-dealing and false friendship that was almost European. "You'd do *that?*" he asked. "After our years of close association?"

Adam nodded. "I'd do just that. I'm not a sentimental man, Christopher. I can't afford to put on a black tie just because you've made a damned fool of yourself. If you have, that is," he added courteously. "Or if you're going to."

Christopher continued to stare in disbelief as the open, boyish face of his old associate uttered the bland, perfidious words. Oddly enough, he was not angry; rather, an agonizing awareness of his own unfair victimization began to balloon within him. It was perhaps not unnatural that in this personal emergency the names of his old standbys, Gandhi and Christ, now flashed with a fresh, unprecedented relevance across his consciousness, for his professional labors had trained him to associate the events of the moment with their historic parallels.

"By God!" he breathed, and shook his head sadly. "I wouldn't have believed it, I *don't* believe it, Adam. . . ."

"Yes, yes, it's hard," said Adam, rather cheerily.

". . . and I suppose I should be furious. I suppose at this moment I should resent your duplicity, and despise you personally. But the fact is, Adam, that I don't, I can't." He paused, and his pale-blue eyes, mirroring some of the candor, the nobility of his feeling, regarded Adam steadily. "I'll tell you what I do feel," he said. "At the moment, more than anything else, I'm—"

"You're hurt," said Adam, rudely shutting off the possibility of sustained, reproachful eloquence. "Forget it, Christopher. There's nothing personal or treacherous about this: I'd say and do the same thing to my own mother. What bothers you is that you've just made a painful discovery: you've suddenly learned that you're in a business that means to stay in business, and if Christopher Usher won't play ball, then Christopher Usher be damned. In short, Christopher, after talking about the American Way for most of your adult life, you've suddenly discovered what it is. It's tough to take, I suppose, but there you have it. Now to be perfectly logical, you have no right to sit on your tail, moaning and running your tongue over your wounds. You're an observer of the contemporary scene; this is part of it. You should be viewing this whole matter with some semblance of professional detachment."

"I don't think I need your advice, Adam," Christopher said coldly. "I don't think that anything you could say would be of much concern to me now; apparently our standards are far too different. And I'm afraid I can't indulge in cheap sneers at such things as personal loyalty, and integrity to one's friends. I've always known you were a cynical man, Adam; I've never known until this moment that you were also a *brutal* one. I'm disappointed, gravely disappointed—"

Adam shrugged. "I'm sorry but not surprised. Sooner or later, most of the people who come into this office confess to a certain disappointment in me. It's all a question of knowing what one has a right to reasonably expect, and I deal with very few realists. And speaking of looking at problems realistically, take a look at your own that way and you'll see that I've done you a rather considerable favor. I've shown you exactly where you stand; I've probably stopped you from playing footsie with a saber-toothed tiger; I may very well have saved your job for you. In that event, you can be grateful to me, and everything can go along just as it was before."

"No," Christopher said bitterly. "No, not just as before, not by a long shot. And I'm afraid you'll have to do without my gratitude. I have no reason to be grateful to you, or to Udolpho either, for that matter. You've talked a lot in the last few minutes, but you've forgotten one most important fact. You've forgotten that instead of talking to just one of the hired help, you were talking to me, to Christopher Usher. That happens to mean something, Adam. It happens to mean that you've been talking to a man who's not exactly helpless. It happens to mean that you've been talking to a man who over the years has established a reputation, a following, a large, believing public. I'm a man in *demand*, and smart advertisers know that. You talk so glibly about my being ruined! Why, if Udolpho should decide to cancel everything tomorrow, I'd be flooded with offers within twenty-four hours. I'd still be Christopher Usher, I'd still be on top of the heap!"

"Wrong again," Adam said. "And wrong on all counts. You said you wanted the facts of life: get ready for a few more. First, you have no idea of just how much you owe to me. Don't for a minute imagine that you just grew, Christopher; you were made, you were the end product of a long, careful and rather expensive campaign. That the end product is you instead of someone else happens to be more or less of an accident; at the time, we needed someone quickly, you were available, and we decided to take a chance. I admit that you had certain rough qualifications: a fair voice, a fluent, superficial approach, a parochial viewpoint on world affairs, and a hearts-and-bowels rather than an intellectual appeal—these were all in your favor, yes. From the beginning I felt that you had possibilities, Christopher; I felt that, brought along properly, you might very well come to command a large following among the unsophisticated, all of whom would see in you the apotheosis of themselves. I felt that you could become—and I say this without meaning to give unnecessary offense—a kind of Quintessential Rube. And so you did, Christopher, but not on your own. Don't ever forget that I selected you, I developed you, I polished you, I promoted you, and I sold you, both to the public and to Udolpho. So much, Christopher, for spontaneous generation; so much for the miracle of your independent rise to power and glory."

It was too much, far too much, to bear; breathing hard, Christopher rose angrily. "Now listen here, Adam!" he cried. "Listen here—"

"No, you listen, Christopher; just for today, I'll do the talking. I want to talk, for example, about this alleged demand for your services. You can forget it; it just doesn't exist. If you split with Udolpho, you're done, a dead duck. And for a number of reasons. You talk about potential sponsors as though they were strawberry boxes, as though they came by the gross. Just how many firms in the United States today do you think there are who'd be willing to spend Udolpho's kind of money on a news commentator? And of those, how many would be willing to touch you with a ten-foot pole once they found that Udolpho had dropped you after nearly nine years? They respect his judgment; they'd reason that something was up; they'd conclude, finally, that Udolpho had figured you had outlived your usefulness. And could you blame them? This is a business of new faces and transient glories, Christopher, and you've been around a long time. What's the mortality rate among commentators, anyway? Remember the bunch who were riding high when you first came along? Every man a god, but how many of the gods are working today? Lowell Thomas? Gabe Heatter? Lewis? Who else? No, Christopher, once the word starts getting around that you may be just a wee bit old-fashioned, that you've started to wear out your welcome, you're cooked, washed up. And that's just what will happen if Udolpho drops you; it can't miss. No sponsor will come near you, and I regret to say that in that melancholy event, we could no longer afford to keep you on the air. If you'll forgive the figure of speech, we can't afford to ride a dead horse. And then what will happen to you? No microphone, no audience; you'll be missed for a week or two, we'll get letters of protest, maybe lots of them, then all of a sudden they'll stop, and you'll be just another ex-god, gone and completely forgotten. Should that occur," he said, by way of concluding on a more genial note; "you're not necessarily through. Presumably you've maintained cordial contact with your former associates on the sports page; you could go back there. Or there is the possibility that you might care to audition for the part of the new Sonny Muscle, although personally I don't recommend it: the vocal requirements of the all-American boy are a bit different from those of the news commentator. You lack a certain falsetto zing. . . ."

Christopher had flung open the door; an ascending rage threatened to mar the dignity of the planned, silently contemptuous exit. He realized this, but he could do nothing about it; flaming in the face of the unprecedented personal affront, he was helpless to avoid the shouted retort which, he knew, was beneath him, beneath his position.

"You'll regret this!" he cried. He shook his fist in supplementary promise of savage retribution. "By God, you'll regret this! I don't have to take anything from you. There are other networks!"

"Try them," advised Adam. "Try them, by all means. You're angry now, but when you calm down, when the bubbles stop popping, go to them and put your best foot forward. Only don't be surprised if you hear a chorus of polite regrets. Word gets around, Christopher; it gets around fast. You'll really do far better to stay put. Hang onto Udolpho with the grip of death; don't let go. And stick with me, with us: old friends are the best—"

The door slammed, viciously, and Adam smiled. It had been, thus far, a day of unaccustomed joys, a rare day when the dictates of business had commanded a course of action congenial to his nature. The attendance at the funeral of the old actor, the blunt, swift, body blows to the self-esteem of a hireling—all this had been good. And added to that was the fact that this time, finally, the hireling had been Christopher. . . . Adam chuckled.

"He'll sweat now," he said, aloud and happily. "Oh, how he'll sweat!"

six

ADAM WAS RIGHT, ALTHOUGH NOT IMMEDIATELY SO. FOR some hours after the meeting, Christopher continued to boil; the fullness of his fury allowed him no time for tormenting speculations upon the probability of future misfortunes. Position, talent, honor, pride—all had been terribly assaulted. He had been treated to a kind of ruthless, cynical frivolity customarily reserved for personalities of lesser dimensions: comedians, quiz masters, radio divines. He had been grossly insulted, and he did not suffer insult gladly. Years before, when, as a sports columnist, he had been widely read and, indeed, even famous within a more constricted circle, he had occasionally been subjected to these painful batterings at his dignity. It had been the habit of his managing editor—a small, sharp-faced man with the air of a raffish mouse—to address him, in the presence of others, by the simple, inaccurate name of "Charlie." More, along with the false diminutive, he would supply an entirely unnecessary identification, whose very superfluousness would serve to further minimize Christopher:

". . . and now I want you to meet Charlie Usher, one of our staff. I'll tell you what Charlie does: he does sports. Been doing them for years. Nice lively style if you like sports. Take a look at his stuff sometime if you get the chance. Now come over here and meet our copy chief. . . ."

It had been bad, it had been mortifying, but it had been long ago. In recent years, insults had come to him rarely. To be sure, in his mail, there were the elaborate sarcasms of undergraduate peace societies, the scabrous epistles from the left, but these did not count. Nothings from nobodies, thin shouts of choler from the jealous and the disaffected, they were dismissable, forgotten in a moment. What was not to be forgotten, however, was this insupportable, face-to-face humiliation at the hands of an equal, a supposed friend. Christopher circled his office with the long strides of the impassioned, realizing in his wrath that the greater the man, the greater the indignity to be endured, and consequently, the greater the revenge required. And here, clearly, was a situation which cried aloud for a vengeance so swift, so savage, so total as to be almost Biblical.

Yet, slowly, a difficulty presented itself. Adam was no fool: he had established himself in his position with care. If he were at all vulnerable, if a chink were to be found in the executive fortifications, one would have to probe, to search, to think. . . . The afternoon wore on, and Christopher, thinking constant, violent thoughts, continued to circle his office. Now and then he paused to pass on some of the fruits of his rage to those about him. He shouted threats of salary reduction and summary dismissal at his secretary; he telephoned Washington and angrily accused his ex-senator tipster of inattention to duty (a reprimand which was as unfair as it was intemperate, for even at the moment of the phone call, the old man had been hard at work in his hotel room, concocting a fresh batch of misinformation for his employer). Meredith had telephoned to welcome her husband home; Christopher had snapped at her; she had hung up. Throughout the afternoon he rushed to his typewriter where—China, Asia, the world and small, domestic animals forgotten in the face of greater issues—he clattered out fierce and feeling sentences on the penetration of the alien spirit of the dictator into the heart of American industry . . .

". . . little men, cheap men, ruthless men, borrowing the techniques of the communists and fascists . . . shouting in tones of command to their fellow citizens . . . highhanded men of cold heart, unfit for the leadership of a free people . . . high time for a reckoning, high time that these self-appointed gods should be made responsible to you, to me . . . should be brought down to earth and brought down hard by the great good common sense, by the native independence of those of us who stand up and shout 'No indeed, sir! We don't play ball that way, not in America!' to these power-crazed few, to these would-be controllers of our hearts, our minds, our spirits and our fates. . . ."

All in all, although something of a departure from his accustomed themes, it promised to be a rousing broadcast. . . .

Afternoon faded into evening, and with it, ever so gradually, Christopher's wrath faded into a sense of frustration, of the bitterest disappointment. Hours of concentration had failed to suggest to him a feasible avenue of retribution; an afternoon of unremitting thought had not revealed the chink in the armor. As he took to the air with his broadcast, he began to wonder if Adam, after all, were not immune to personal revenge? It was a melancholy thought with which to begin a broadcast, and it was a tribute to his powers as an artist that despite his disappointment, as he read aloud the words which only a few hours before had poured smoking from red wounds, he was able to communicate to his audience something of his original, unwatered distemper.

After the broadcast, however, he suffered a further letdown. If Adam were indeed invulnerable, there was nothing for it but to swallow humiliation, acknowledge defeat, do nothing. The position was intolerable; he left the studio hastily and drove without purpose through the streets of the city for more than an hour. In his present mood, he was not prepared to face his wife, and even the plump, supple charms of Lura were insufficient to draw him from his own sad self. It was some time before his thoughts began to expand beyond the limits of personal vindication to include the problem of his own professional future. He had been so preoccupied with Adam that he had forgotten Udolpho; now, suddenly, he began to consider his broadcasts, to reflect upon the possibilities of maintaining his position at its present level of influence and rich reward. It was at this point, finally, that the disappointment which had followed wrath was in turn succeeded by doubt; it was at this point that the hints, the disquieting warnings which had been cloaked by the curtain of his rage now began to weave themselves into a visible and disturbing pattern; it was at this point that, as Adam had foretold, and despite the faint chill of the early autumn night, Christopher began, ever so slightly, to sweat. . . .

When, eventually, he reached his home, he was in such a state of self-doubt and uncertainty as he had not known since the beginning of his broadcasting career. In the library, Meredith was waiting for him.

"Christopher, I want to talk to you."

"I know," he said wearily. "About this afternoon on the phone, Meredith: I'm sorry. I was extremely upset by something. I apologize, I was wrong, but I'd rather not talk any more about it right now. I'm tired, very tired." To indicate the depths of his weariness, he added, "I won't have anything for dinner. Just a little buttermilk."

Meredith looked at him curiously; prepared for argument, she was disarmed by this pale dietary demand. "Aren't you feeling well?" she asked. "Were you ill on your trip?"

"No, no, nothing like that. I had an excellent trip, one of the best." Mysteriously he said, "It's what has occurred since the trip that's left me tired. Tired and disappointed. Is the general in, by the way?"

"No, he's speaking to the Hi-Y tonight. But what on earth—"

"Good," said Christopher. "He's a remarkable man, but I just don't feel up to him tonight. I think I'll go to bed, Meredith; I don't think I'll even have any buttermilk. I may feel more like myself in the morning."

Meredith took him by the hand. "Come over here and sit down," she commanded. "We might just as well talk this out right now." Her slight anger was gone, having given way to concern; she pulled her husband, unresisting, over to a couch and sat down beside him. "Now I know something's wrong," she said, speaking in the maternal, half-playful manner with which, in the past, she had sometimes coaxed him from occasional moods. "You fold up so docilely. What is it, Christopher? Is it all this salary business you preferred not to tell me about?"

"Ah, the salary," he said sadly. For the moment, he had forgotten the secret which he had so carefully guarded from her; now that it was out, it did not seem to matter at all. "The general told you," he said accusingly. Quite simply, it was just one more example of the untrustworthiness of a friend, another demonstration of the perfidy which surrounded him like the very air he breathed.

"Yes, he told me, in a rather roundabout way. Don't blame him, though; I really wormed it out of the old dear. But why didn't you tell me? Why bother to keep it a secret at all? That's what I couldn't understand. And now you come back home up to your neck in gloom; I haven't seen you this low in years." Quietly, she said, "Please tell me what's wrong. I want to know."

"About the salary," he said. "I didn't tell you about it for a very good reason." For just an instant, he had a wild impulse to tell her the truth, to confess all, to reveal the fact of Lura, to receive, in his misery, the absolution of his wife; such was his weakened condition that conscience rose dangerously and struggled briefly before being overcome by prudence. "I didn't tell you because I wasn't sure of it myself. I wanted to wait until it actually came through, I wanted to surprise you. Now," he said, returning to unhappy truth, "it begins to look as if I may have to surprise you in a different way." He told her the story: the contract negotiations, the meeting with Keisler, the telephone conversation with Udolpho, the final, shattering encounter with Adam Flair. It was a long story; he told it dolefully and completely, and when he had finished he looked up at his wife, his pale-blue eyes bathed in melancholy resignation.

"And that's the reward, Meredith," he said sadly, "of a lifetime of good works and honest endeavor!"

Meredith was indignant, sympathetic, encouraging. "I've never trusted Adam Flair," she said. "I've always felt that there was something tricky about a man of his age with that innocent, unlined face. He's the coldest man I've ever met . . . you poor dear, it must have been simply awful! Isn't there some way you can do something about him?"

Christopher smiled mournfully. "Apparently not," he said. "I've thought it over all afternoon, and there doesn't seem to be any way. The unscrupulous manage to guard themselves well, Meredith. They're prepared for treachery in others." As a corollary, he analyzed himself. "My fault is that I'm decent. My fault is that I like to trust people, to believe in them, to regard them as being fundamentally honest. In Adam's case I was wrong. He fooled me and I admit it." To mitigate the severity of this self-condemnation he added, "Although I must say that my mistake was at least one of the heart, and not of the head."

"I know, dear," she said soothingly. "They're much the better."

"Yes," he said. He slumped back on the couch, his eyes

closed, and began to speak of himself with a certain sad grandiloquence.

"All my life I've done my best to deal fairly, honorably with people. I don't suppose it would be an exaggeration to say that in a material sense, at least, I've always given far more than I've received. That's not a complaint: I've been in the position to give, and I've always been happy to do so. As a matter of fact I've regarded it as an obligation. I've always felt that if I had been given certain special talents, it was my duty, so to speak, to share the fruits of those talents with those less fortunate. Just from a purely financial point of view, Meredith, you have no idea of how many people I've helped over the little rough spots, the difficulties of life. And I've always done these things willingly, gladly, *silently*. . . ."

"Yes, dear, I know you have. I've always thought it rather wonderful of you." She saw with relief that the crisis, though undoubtedly serious, was not as grave as she had at first feared. Experience had taught her that with her husband, the danger signal was the desolate eye combined with the absence of speech; in the vigorously flowing tongue, no matter how mournful the subject, there was contained the promise of recovery.

Christopher continued to pursue the vein of *noblesse oblige*:

". . . and yet I've always felt that the material assistance, although important, was secondary. I've always felt that what mattered, what really mattered, was the knowledge, the hope, the consolation I could bring to them on my broadcasts. These people are baffled, mystified, discouraged by the world today; they want to know what it all means, they want to know if there's a way out of the darkness, they want to know if everything's doomed or if life is really worth living. And that's where I came in, Meredith. I came in to bring them the news, but more than that, to tell them what the news means. I came in to show them that there are bright spots all around them, to show them that the world isn't such a bad old place after all. I gave them leadership, guidance, assurance: that was my job to do and I think I can say I've done it well. I wish you could see my mail every day of the week. I wish you could see the pitifully grateful letters from hundreds, *thousands* of people who look up to me, who *depend* upon me! That's why this is no laughing matter. That's why, when a greedy little gangster can cut these people off from the sound of my voice, it becomes something sinister, something horrible! My God, here we are in America, and in the twentieth century, and with such things going on we might as well be living in the . . . the . . ." he gestured wildly, groping for an appropriately debased period in history ". . . the Renaissance!" he concluded triumphantly, and sank back once again, pausing for sympathy, encouragement, breath.

"I wonder if it's really worth all this, Christopher," Meredith said gently. "As a matter of fact, I've wondered the same thing before. After all, we managed to get by fairly well before you went on the radio. It was a bit different, of course; you may not have had the same responsibilities you have now, but you had enough, and I'm not sure, really, that it wasn't a better life. What I'm trying to say," she said, "is that I'm not at all sure that this radio career has been an unmixed blessing. I don't want to be sentimental, but I think that we've both been changed by it, and I don't think it's made us any happier. Haven't you felt that too, Christopher? Once or twice, away down deep?"

Christopher stared at her. "My God," he said, frowning, "this is a fine time for jokes!"

For a moment Meredith said nothing; then, shrugging slightly, she smiled. "All right, Christopher," she said. "I really wasn't joking, but never mind that. I suppose the main thing is what you plan to do now."

Christopher waved hopelessly. "That's the big question, the sixty-four dollar question, isn't it? If it were anybody else but Udolpho, I'd go right to him and appeal to his sense of justice, of fair play; I'd try to point out to him just what it is that he's doing. But that's no good here. Udolpho's a Sicilian, and historically speaking, they're a people who prefer to do things the inhuman way."

"Do you know what I think? If everything you've told me is *all* that has happened, I think it's entirely possible that you may be making too much of this."

"Too *much!*" he cried. He slumped further back, in

boneless despair. "So you're deserting me too," he groaned bitterly.

"No, of course I'm not. But isn't it possible that you might be jumping to conclusions? You sometimes do, you know. Especially when you're depressed; you manage to talk yourself into things. And I honestly think that this is one of those times. Now really, Christopher," she said persuasively, "what evidence have you that Udolpho means to cancel? Actually, not a single bit. This man Keisler and his rumors, Adam's being nasty, a telephone conversation with Udolpho—they're not exactly conclusive, are they?"

Christopher sighed. "They're signposts. Signposts that point in one direction. You're not experienced in these matters, Meredith; you don't know the radio business as I do. One thing leads to another. One and one make two, and that's all there is to it. I've seen it happen time and time again, and now," he said, smiling sadly, "they're making two for me!"

It was like the wistful climax to a lachrymose popular song: *And now they're making two for me*; irresistibly the notion occurred to Meredith and it was with some difficulty that she shook it off and said, "Now Christopher, please listen to me, just for a minute. Let's review the whole matter again; let's see if it's really as serious as you think it is."

In the face of negative gestures of apathy and despair, she set about the business of reinflating her husband's spirits. It was not a particularly formidable operation; she had done it before in the rare intervals of despondency. In skeletal form, it consisted in telling him that he had done well; it was a pep talk. More elaborately, it involved a knowing a detailed recitation of his personal and professional achievements. To eliminate any difficulty of communication, this recitation was made, as nearly as possible, in the same words which he himself used when describing his life and works. It was bracing therapy; he rarely failed to respond. Now, like a pilot, weak and lackluster in thin upper air, suddenly supplied with saving draughts of oxygen, Christopher began to breathe deeply, to revive at the heartening words. He began to sit upright, to nod his head in agreement, to participate in monosyllabic affirmation.

"Yes, yes," he said, several times. Then, as truth followed truth, as the words which he had so often spoken in self-evaluation now came back to him from another, it seemed as though he were seeing himself for the first time, as though he were gazing, at last, into a relentless, multi-dimensional mirror which revealed him fully, frankly, magnificently. "Yes, yes, YES!" he cried, and as the great, life-giving fog of confidence swept over him, he felt a sudden flush of shame at having forgotten, even for a few hours, just who and what he was.

"You're right," he exclaimed, rising. "My God, how right you are, Meredith!" In the quick accession of joy at being confronted with his own perfections, he grabbed her about the waist and whirled her about in a series of clumsy dance steps. As always, after one of these swift shiftings of emotional gears, he felt air-borne in his happiness; cares and dangers no doubt remained, but they were shrunken threats to the giant who now two-stepped in triumph across the room. "I'll show them," he vowed as he danced. "I'll make the broadcasts so good they won't dare do anything. I'll fight them and I'll win. Easily!"

Somewhat breathless at this athletic result of her efforts, Meredith said, "Then it's all right now? No more change and decay in all around I see?"

"No, no, no more of that." Pausing, he took his wife's hand and patted it affectionately. "Out of the doldrums," he said, and laughed loudly. "My God, Meredith, when you come to think of it, how silly I was. If I managed to fight Stalin, Hitler and Mussolini all through the dim, dark years, I guess I can hold my own with Bernie Udolpho!"

Arm in arm, he walked with his wife to the stairs. He felt a profound gratitude toward her for realizing his strength, for reminding him of his position, for helping to snap him out of a depression which had been so unseemly, so without cause. At the foot of the stairs, he paused to voice this gratitude. Suddenly solemn, he lifted her chin and looked down at her.

"There are times, Meredith," he said gravely, "when I ought to stop and give thanks to heaven that at least one of us has the good sense to realize when I'm being so damned unnecessarily humble!"

Later that night, lying in bed, reviewing the events of the turbulent day, this feeling of gratitude increased, and thinking of his sustained infidelity with Lura, he grew remorseful.

"Cheap, cheap," he muttered to himself, and resolved not to see Lura again; at least, not for some time. . . .

His resolve held, to some extent; it was nearly twenty-four hours before he made his way to Lura's apartment. As he opened the door he was troubled with the faint stabbings of guilt; these persisted to lend an unaccustomed quality of restraint to his first ardors. Lura, surprised, stared at him reproachfully; not a proud woman, there were nevertheless certain areas of activity in which she felt her honor to be at stake.

"Chris baby! And after all this time away from Lura!" Wounded, she wriggled petulantly and accused him of unhealthy prudery. "Sometimes," she said, "I think you're nothing but a *Pilgrim!*"

"Puritan," he corrected, automatically. "You mean Puritan, not Pilgrim, Lura. And in any case, you're quite wrong. It's just that occasionally I have so many things on my mind that I may seem a bit abstracted, a bit remote. . . ."

"My Chris baby is such a busy man, always *thinking*. That's what I love about him. I love a man that thinks. But sometimes I wish Chris baby would think more about his Lura. Sometimes I wonder if he's *happy-happy*. . . ."

"Yes, of course I'm happy." But the words, he knew, failed to approach his usual standard of passionate affirmation; to make good the deficiency, he gave her a few supplementary pinches; he tried to summon a wanton smile. The effort was not successful; his conscience still twinging, he reflected gloomily that for those of strong moral fiber, life was far more difficult than for the frankly libidinous. Fearing that Lura might not appreciate the delicate nature of such musings, he decided to blame his unease on the worries of business.

"The fact is that I've just come through a crisis. A considerable crisis." Eliminating all mention of Meredith, he told her of the threats made against his position, of his refusal to be daunted, of the certainty of his ultimate victory. Lura listened alertly to every word.

"Then it's all right?" she asked, in an odd, brisk tone. "I mean," she said hastily, "my Chris baby is sure?"

"Naturally I'm sure." He looked at her curiously; the quick, pouncing question had surprised him. "What do you mean?" A terrible suspicion sprang up suddenly: did the faithlessness of friends extend even here? "What do you mean?" he repeated loudly. "Do you mean that it would make such a big difference to you? Do you mean that if I were no longer a figure of national influence, so to speak, that your feelings might change? Is that what you mean?"

"Chris baby! So cruel! No, no, no. . . ."

He continued to look at her with some mistrust. "I hope

not," he said slowly. "I sincerely hope not, Lura. I must say that your first reaction seemed a bit peculiar."

"No, no, Chris baby!" Suddenly springing into the center of the room, she stood there, oddly transformed: her feet spread wide apart, her legs flexed slightly outward at the knees, she seemed to crouch in semi-frog posture. An expression of extraordinary vacuity crossed her face. Her eyes closed, and her voice emerged in a series of uninflected grunts, roughly approximating the speech of the stage Negro. Lura was acting.

"When Surara give her heart to one," she said cryptically, "she give dat heart forever."

"What?" said Christopher, startled.

"My *picture*, Chris baby," she said, somewhat impatiently. "When I was the White Ranee. Her name was Surara and she loved her man through *everything*." She pointed to herself, indicating that this portrayal of Sumatran fidelity was not without symbolism; then, once more closing her eyes, she continued to re-create her greatest, indeed her only, screen triumph. "Dey can cut off his hands, dey can cut off his feet, dey can pull out all his teet," she chanted, the lyrical words now stirring her to perceptible inflection, "but dey can't take Jim from Surara! It was a *wonderful* picture, Chris baby," she said sadly, "but they never released it. That cheap bastard Xavier Kornbloom fixed *that*." She spoke venomously, for the memory of that coarse and burly figure in the screening room, who had alternately spat, groaned and pared his

146

nails throughout her best scenes, and who, with a few ruthless and profane comments had stilled a career at its birth, was not a happy one. For an instant she was depressed; then recalling the necessities of the moment, she banished past disappointments and flung herself into Christopher's lap.

"So *suspicious*," she crooned, stroking his cheek. "So *mean* to Lura. Shame on Chris baby!"

"I was too quick," he admitted. "Too hasty. I apologize, Lura." He was contrite: the straightforward, primitive profession of loyalty by the frank, healthy creature now bouncing about on his knees left him ashamed of his suspicions. The sense of his unfairness to her diminished his reluctance for play; plaguing conscience was stilled by the knowledge that he must, after all, make amends. It was nothing but his own largeness of spirit that erased, now, the disquieting image of his wife; he reached out and chucked Lura under her smooth, soft chin.

"Yum yum yum," said the adversary of Hitler, Mussolini, Stalin and Bernie Udolpho. "Yummy YUM yum yum. . . ."

Much later, he went home happy, a song on his lips. But Lura, left alone, was unusually thoughtful. It was a perilous world in which she lived, and she lived, if not by her wits, at least on the strength of past experience. While on the one hand she did not actually distrust Christopher, did not really disbelieve his optimistic assurances, on the other she had the profound respect of her profession for the uncertainties of employment. Moreover, looking meditatively at her hand, she saw that the promised sapphire was not yet there. It was all most difficult, and across her broad and ordinarily placid features crept a few strange lines, bred by the unfamiliar process of cerebration. She had to make up her mind, for of one thing and one thing only was she absolutely sure: a little girl, alone in the world, had to take care of herself. . . .

seven

CHRISTOPHER BEGAN AT ONCE TO FULFILL HIS PROMISE OF making his broadcasts even better than before. Quite soberly, he realized the formidable proportions of the task; no one knew better than he the difficulty of improving upon the already impeccable. Nevertheless, he was willing to try: he felt that within him there were vast reserves as yet untapped, and all that he asked in the way of co-operation was that the raw material of human behavior would not, in this moment of crisis, fail him.

It did not: fortunately there were two small wars which gave no indication of early armistice. Both of these were of sufficient size to warrant the presence of American troops; when they had begun, some time ago, Christopher had predicted their end in a matter of days, hours. As the days had lengthened into weeks, and the weeks into months, his prophecies became no less confident if somewhat less specific. Phrases such as "ultimate victory," and "in the not-far-distant future" now cropped up regularly in his heartening addresses. Nightly he deplored the carnage, yet no one on the American scene saw more clearly or depicted more warmly the glorious aspects of this human adventure. It was from this hour of evil trial, as he saw it, that invaluable lessons in brotherhood were forged. He had never seen a battlefield, but he was not without imagination, and often he drew for his listeners moving miniatures of the manner in which men, dying, paused to think, to gain in strength. . . .

". . . the doomed plane plummeting to earth, its heroic mission accomplished, its work done forever. And on that plane the three American boys who stand in death a symbol to us the living. On that plane those three young men who, dying for their land before their time, clasp hands and wait, clasp hands and silently speak to us all the last great lesson of their lives. 'This is the way it's done,' they say. 'This is the way it's done, you folks at home. Not in hatred, in fear, or in suspicion, but in courage, in understanding, in friendship. One for all and all for one: that is the legacy which we the dying leave to you. Remember it well!' Yes, on that plane the three young Americans whose names will be remembered as long as history is read: Murphy the Catholic, Whitman the Protestant, Epstein the Jew, united in their belief that their country, that right, that freedom will and must prevail, and willing to die for that belief. And to those men I take the liberty of replying for all of us: 'Sleep well, soldiers, sleep well. May this mighty nation of ours profit by your example. . . ."

As he pronounced these words of valediction to the departed airmen, words which he himself had written, he became choked with emotion, and it was with difficulty that he could continue. Fortunately, the next item helped to pull him out of it; it was about trained worms. A scientist on the West Coast was laboriously instructing young angleworms to crawl through a maze, determining whether or not they might one day slither through the proper channels to freedom. In the experiment, Christopher could glimpse exciting new horizons. . . .

". . . a question for you, a question for me: can these trained worms *learn*? Have they, like you, like me, an *intellect* . . . ?"

Still, despite the rich variety of global experiences with which he found himself surrounded, despite the passion with which he threw himself into his labors, despite his ringing expressions of confidence, first uncertainty, then worry, returned. For somehow, during the next few days, his status at the network had been altered—mysteriously, unobtrusively, but unmistakably.

There had been a series of incidents which had brought this unpleasant truth home. . . .

First, there had been the dramatic and offensive episode of the janitor. Early in the week, as Christopher had finished his broadcast, he had been preparing to leave the building when he had met one of the night janitors. Christopher had seen him often before: a long, glum man who prowled about the building each night, alternately emptying ashtrays and piecing together the torn letters found in executive wastebaskets. Comfortingly deferential in the presence of authority, he had always greeted Christopher with an obeisant little bow and muttered phrases of respect. On this night, Christopher had given him the usual large, manorial wave; to his astonishment, the janitor had responded with a jaunty flip of his hand. "Whaddaya say, Mac," he had said, familiarly.

Whaddaya say! And *Mac!* It was an incredible violation of the building's caste system; too stupefied to move or speak, Christopher could only stare after the man, sauntering so insolently down the corridor. Could the man have failed to recognize him? Was he ill, drunk? And yet he had seemed quite normal . . . puzzled, Christopher had left the building, still wondering.

On the following morning, there had occurred the second of the curious incidents. In the barbershop, he had had a haircut, a shave; looking carefully at himself in the mirror, he said, "I think that will be all, Frank."

"Yes sir, Mr. Usher. You want that put on your bill?"

"Yes, of course. As usual."

"Okay. I'll mail that to you at the studio, will I, Mr. Usher?"

Christopher stared at him. "Naturally you'll mail it to the studio. You've been mailing it there for the past nine years, haven't you? Where else would you mail it?"

"That's right, sir," said the barber, smiling brilliantly. "Whatever you say, Mr. Usher."

Christopher had left the barber shop, annoyed. Upstairs, in his office, his secretary said apologetically. "Some of these letters should have come in a good deal sooner, I'm afraid. They must have been misdirected to another department."

"Misdirected? How could they be misdirected? My name is on every one of them, and to the best of my knowledge I'm the only Christopher Usher in this network. It's never happened before."

"The service has been a little sloppy lately," said his secretary. "I've noticed it."

There was no misdirection about the bill from the barber shop, however; it arrived the first thing that afternoon.

They were little things, but their cumulative effect was unsettling. Against his will, and with mounting alarm, Christopher was forced to conclude that something was wrong. The atmosphere had changed; he saw it on every side. At no time did he again encounter any such abrupt volte-face as that of the janitor: subordinates remained polite, equals or almost-equals, continued to greet him

153

with the mixture of joviality and covert suspicion usual among the high-salaried in a competitive industry. Yet the change was there . . . for one thing, there was the gradual awareness that he was being avoided. There had been a sharp drop in the number of those who came to him for advice, wisdom, favors. Even the indefatigable Mr. Chan, once the urbane, amber constant of his waiting room, had not appeared for days. One afternoon Christopher came upon him quite by chance, a casual encounter in the hall. He had been on a tour of the building, testing reactions to himself; returning moodily to his office, he saw a door open along the corridor. From it, in a sequence of familiar, gracefully compliant bows, backed a slender figure in a frock coat.

"Good afternoon, Mr. Chan," Christopher said accusingly, for the door from which the Chinese had so submissively emerged was marked with the competitive legend: SYDNEY DUNSANY: TOMORROW'S NEWS BEFORE IT HAPPENS.

"Ah, it is Mr. Usher!" The man, Christopher noted, was shameless: on the old Oriental face was neither confusion nor a becoming embarrassment, but only the delighted smile of an old friend. "How good it is to see you," he said happily. "One's day is dull, without event, and then comes such a delightful happening as this!"

"Yes. I haven't seen you for quite some time."

Mr. Chan's face grew sad. "How distressing it has been

for me," he said. "I have been away. Far away. In the service of my unhappy country."

"I see. I hadn't heard that you'd gone anywhere, but that doesn't matter, I suppose. Did you have a profitable talk with Mr. Dunsany?"

"Ah, Mr. Dunsany. A nice young man. A youth in point of years, but with ideas of excellence. He is interested, so interested, in China. In a small way," Mr. Chan said modestly, "I have been able to help him, to inform him. He is a most receptive young man. Most highly educated. From Connecticut Agricultural College, I believe."

Christopher smiled bitterly. "I only hope your efforts haven't been wasted. By that I mean that I wouldn't think that Mr. Dunsany was in any position to advance your cause, so to speak. You see, Mr. Chan, unlike myself, Dunsany doesn't command a nation-wide audience. Actually, relatively few people hear him; he's regarded around here as a purely local commentator. As a matter of fact, although I don't make a practice of listening to him, I believe that he's not allowed to discuss world affairs. I believe that he's strictly limited to state and local politics."

"Yes, yes, that is how it has been." Mr. Churchill Chan's smile remained, perpetual and ineradicable beneath soft, uninformative eyes. "One hears, however," he murmured, "that he is shortly to expand, to flower. One hears that he is destined for larger matters in the near future. *Much* larger." The old face shone with luminous

155

benevolence. "One likes to help young people to rise," he said. "It is a duty." A large silver watch appeared from some interior recess of his clothing and Mr. Churchill Chan's eyes widened with surprise, regret. "So late," he said sadly. Trim little feet began to move smoothly backward; his slim body bobbed in flexible, courteous inclinations. "At the moment one would linger most, it becomes necessary to go. A servant's time, alas, is not his own," he sighed, the agile bromides of an ancient land buttering his swift retreat. "One day soon," he said, nodding, "we must talk. We have many things to say. Until then, farewell." Quickly he dissolved around a corner, a melting miracle of evanescence.

Incidents of this description, regularly punctuating the routine of the succeeding days, were not without an erosive effect. Christopher grew increasingly nervous; he thought, oddly enough, of Leonard Keisler. Sometimes, he knew, within an organization such as this, there was an uncanny, animal awareness of things to come; it was like the rats and the sinking ship. In his tenure at the network, he had seen more than one fall from the heights preceded by an office boy's wink, a smug secretarial smile, the little signs that the Word Had Gone Around. Had it, possibly, gone around for *him*? He could not believe it, and yet, confronted by the diurnal behavior of his associates, he felt suddenly chilled. . . .

The growing tenseness invaded even his home. In the continued presence of the general he found an increasing source of irritation. There was no doubt of it, he decided: eminent warrior though the old man might be, he did not wear well in the prolonged association of the library. What Christopher required at the moment was a confidant, and the general, unhappily, was the worst of listeners. Informed of Christopher's trials, he was unfailingly sympathetic; his sympathy took the form of little nods of understanding, and comfortable, rather lengthy tales of his own valiant survivals of adversity. It was this last which Christopher found particularly infuriating.

"But I can't help feeling that you don't quite realize the importance, the *seriousness* of the situation, Beak. I know that you've had difficulties, probably many of them, but it seems to me that this is on an altogether different level. After all, we are on the brink of a global crisis, very possibly another world war. It's a situation where, more than anything else, the country needs cool heads, impartial judgment, expert advice. And in spite of this, there's an excellent chance that my voice may soon be removed from the arena of public discussion. . . ."

"How well I know what you are going through," said the general, smiling wisely. "The main thing, of course, is to keep up your courage. I've been in jams, really *bad* jams, and nothing but sheer courage and my own superior knowledge of tactics pulled me through. I particularly recall one evening in May, 1918. I was a major then, young and full of beans. We were situated just north of Verdun, about ten miles west of the Meuse, and the outlook was dark. The Hun was all around us, and our communications, my dear Christopher, had been *completely cut off. . . ."*

He went on, the old voice holding in loving recapture the endless details of a story of hardship, valor and hairbreadth escape. Christopher listened impatiently to this tale of ancient derring-do. Comparatively, he thought sourly, it was trivial, it was small potatoes; almost jealously, he considered once again the immensity of his own predicament.

". . . after which we turned and fell upon the enemy with a vengeance! I myself fought with a fury of which I had never believed myself capable. It was one of the turning points of the war, and I," said the general, with a modest little wave, "was made a *lieutenant-colonel on the spot!* And the moral of that story, Christopher, may be summed up in one word: *pluck.* Pluck," he repeated thoughtfully, and rose from his chair, summoned from the past by the urgencies of the present. "Shall we adjourn to the kitchen for a late-evening snack? Some scrambled eggs, perhaps? With a bit of bacon? Or possibly . . . as I passed by the refrigerator earlier in the day, I thought I caught just a glimpse of some of that delicious Polish ham. . . ."

Christopher complained to Meredith.

"How long is he planning to stay? Hasn't he said anything about leaving?"

"Not a word. For all I know, he may very well plan on staying through Christmas. In that event there's the problem of a suitable gift. *I* don't know what one gives to a general, do you?"

"That isn't funny," Christopher said fretfully. "It's long past the point of being amusing. He's a military man and his country is in a crisis; I should think he'd be anxious to get into the thick of things, to play an active role. Instead, he seems perfectly content to sit back here and talk. I appreciate the fact that he's a remarkable man with a distinguished career behind him, but I simply can't go on listening to him night after night. I happen to have troubles of my own, serious troubles . . . are you listening to me, Meredith?"

"Yes, Christopher, I'm listening." It was the truth, but it was also true that for the past few days the listening had come harder. There was a new note in her husband's complaints, almost hysterical. She had ceased trying to cheer him; her efforts were strangely powerless before this dank cloud of depression which had settled irremovably upon him. A neutral factor, she waited now for the day of decision; whatever came, she could deal with the resulting fortunes or disasters. In the meantime, in this period of taut anticipation, it could not be denied that she found her husband singularly trying.

"If it bores you, you certainly don't have to listen. It's simply that I thought that you might have some vague interest in what happens to me." A dereliction in the home, his own wife suspected of indifference: objectively considering himself, he thought that he deserved far better than he got. Somewhat sentimentally, he thought of how much of his time, talent, affection, indeed, of his *life*, he had given to his wife, and under such circumstances it was difficult for him to avoid self-pity.

Then, early one afternoon, as the deadline with Udolpho drew inexorably closer, another blow fell—of quite a different kind, from an unexpected quarter. He was in his car, returning from the reluctant performance of one of the many subsidiary duties to which his position made him liable. A soft drink company had sponsored a nation-wide essay contest for young people on the subject of Americanism; the winner had been chosen, and Christopher had been requested to present the award. In his present disheveled state of mind, this ordinarily exhilarating event had promised to be the dullest of chores; still, conscious always of his public responsibilities, he had gone. The winner had proved to be an eleven-year-old girl of truculent appearance, whose essay, *Would Stalin Love Me?*, was surprisingly good, especially when one considered that her father had previously written very little for competitions of this kind.

The ceremony had been thoroughly disagreeable. The hall had been packed with early adolescents in compulsory attendance, and although Christopher prided himself on his ability to establish contact with the young, today, as from the stage he had gazed down at the sea of inattentive faces, and had listened to the mingled snuffling and scraping and muttering that had persisted throughout his address, he had been filled with a distaste for them all.

Little hoodlums, he had thought bitterly, and he had punished them by speaking for only twenty-five minutes.

Now, riding back to the studio, he drove recklessly, twisting the steering wheel with quick, savage jerks, almost as though the inanimate plastic surface had become the head and shoulders of one of the hooting youngsters. A stop light flashed suddenly; he came to a shuddering halt. It was a long light; as it refused to change, he began to gaze around, aimlessly, discontentedly, and it was then that he saw Lura.

She was walking rapidly toward a taxi on the other side of the intersection; to his utter stupefaction, he saw that she was not without escort. A slight, swarthy man of rather furtive aspect trailed her closely; their arms linked together, he had the appearance of being led, and Lura, twisting slightly to talk to him, was smiling, vivacious. Openmouthed, Christopher watched as they entered a taxi together and drove off; it took the raucous horns signaling the change of the light to blast him into full consciousness, to stir him to a furious awareness of what he had actually seen. Roaring into gear, he tried to find the taxi, to follow it; he was too late. He returned hastily to the studio and called Lura's apartment; the phone rang and continued to ring. He surged with rage, jealousy: was it possible that Lura, too . . . ? And, if so, had she deliberately chosen this hour of his torment to cheat, betray, dishonor? It was agonizing, insupportable; throughout the long afternoon he called her apartment continually; no one answered. It was perhaps the supreme triumph of self-discipline that, although torn in two by the distraction of passion, he was able to write, arrange and deliver an acceptable broadcast, although such was the intensity of his feeling that in the delivery, he twice came perilously close to mispronunciation.

The broadcast over, he hastened to Lura's apartment, uncertain of what—or *whom?*—he would find. He found Lura, alone. Steeled for conflict, he was relieved, but slightly let down. She was asleep on the divan; the muted light from a single table lamp revealed her in delicious curvilinear relaxation. As she slept she smiled gently, and to add the general impression of innocent serenity, a novel by Lloyd Douglas lay folded across her bosom. Insensitive even to this, Christopher woke her rudely.

"Chris baby!" She sat up, rubbing her eyes, stretching in a sequence of jungle movements. "So red in the *face!*" she said, examining him.

"I'm flattered that you're here," Christopher said hoarsely. "I'm tremendously flattered that you could find time for me in your busy day. I suppose I should thank you, thank you for coming to spend a few moments alone with me. That is, if we *are* alone!"

"Chris baby, something's *wrong!* I know it, I can tell it by your voice. Has Lura *done* something . . . ?"

"I saw you!" he blurted. He had meant to be crafty; it

162

had been his intention to trap her through her own admissions, but the accusation, held in through the long agonizing hours, had exploded from him. "I saw you in the city this afternoon. And you weren't alone, Lura. Oh no . . . you were far from being alone!"

"Chris, baby!" Long, plump white arms flung themselves about his neck; he sought to disengage himself from the faithless embrace, but she held on. "Jealous baby," she cooed. "Listen to Lura. Can't a girl go shopping with her big brother?"

"Big brother!" Christopher laughed harshly. "My God, you must think I'm a prize imbecile to believe that. Big brother!"

"But it's true, Chris baby! I swear it's true. Look," she said, freeing one arm and reaching for her handbag, "I'll show you the proof." She scrambled through the bag and came up triumphantly with a small rectangular bit of paper. "Look, Chris baby," she said, handing it to him, "a family picture!"

It was a photograph, evidently taken some years before. A sullen-faced old woman stood in front of a dismal frame house; to her left stood Lura, smiling and dominant; to the right was the man with whom he had seen her that afternoon.

"I don't see where that proves a thing. . . ."

"Turn it over, Chris baby!"

On the back had been inscribed the words, in Lura's large, childish scrawl: *Momma and her family, 1942.*

163

"There, you *see*? That's a picture of Momma and Brother and me. It was taken at Momma's farm. Now aren't you *shame-shame*, Chris baby?"

If it was not conclusive proof, it was at least evidence of a sort; Christopher's voice became less accusing. "I *want* to believe you, Lura. God knows I want to believe you. I don't recall having heard you even mention this brother before. . . ."

"Mmm, no. Brother's so unhappy. You see, he's not *normal*. . . ."

"Not normal? You mean he's insane?"

"No, not *insane*. Poor Brother just hasn't normal *instincts*. You know what I mean," she said delicately. "I don't like to talk about these things with you, Chris baby. So unhappy. . . ."

"Oh." Staring doubtfully at the photograph, he said, "He doesn't even look like you. I mean, there doesn't appear to be the slightest family resemblance. He looks foreign, rather . . . well, rather Jewish. . . ."

"Chris baby! *Now* who's anti-Semitic?" She tugged at him and pulled him down to her; playfully, she bit the lobe of his ear with white little teeth. "It's just that he's black-Irish. A lot of them look like that. You know I was Irish, Chris baby; my maiden name," she murmured, thinking long-ago thoughts, "was Pendergast. *Believe* Lura, Chris baby; she's good for you!"

"I suppose so," he said unhappily. Betrayed on all sides—he thought now of Meredith, of late so insufficiently attentive—he had to trust some one; Lura, at least, was not guilty of indifference. Besides, the lapse into the diction of intolerance had alarmed him, diverted him somewhat from his wrath; the unguarded tongue in that direction spelled professional death.

"I'm sorry if I seemed suspicious," he said. "But you must admit that appearances were against you. . . ."

"Mmm, so *jumpy* lately, Chris baby. *Trust* Lura. . . ."

"I know. You see, I've been worrying, Lura. Worrying far too much." Pale-blue eyes reached out, imploring consolation. "You're not in a position to realize it, Lura," he said, "but these are terrible times for honest men in high places."

"Mmm, bad old times. Forget them, Chris baby. Let Lura *help* you. . . ."

Lura helped. In the blissful anesthesia of the nubile embrace, worry was dulled, cares partially forgotten. But later, when Christopher was alone, they came swarming back in force, prodding, goading, smothering him, rendering sleep impossible. Miserably, he reflected that for woes of his dimensions, Lura was an imperfect anodyne. She was good within her limitations, yes; but the thought of five million souls, dangling free and unsupported, groping for his resonant baritone wisdom . . . this constituted a disaster far beyond the powers of Lura to repair.

Thus it was that as the week wore on and pressure mounted, Christopher, humbling himself, decided at last to investigate the consolations of religion. . . .

"Actually, Father, I'm fairly well acquainted with your

church and its aims." He had chosen Catholicism: he would commit himself to nothing, merely probe, search, and then, possibly later, he might, given reasonable concessions, join. He could do worse; there was about the church a size, an impressiveness, a splendor which might very well be adequate to his needs. Moreover, there was the advantage of propinquity: the small Jesuit church stood not a block from his home. "Very well acquainted, as a matter of fact."

"I see," said the old priest. He was puzzled and not entirely pleased by this late-night visit. A tall, silvery, rather dreamy man of scholarly temperament, he had been hard at work preparing another of his Sunday sermons on the liturgies of the East. This week it was to be the liturgy of the Armenians; he had hardly begun to trace it from the Greek liturgy of St. Basil as used at Caesarea when the arrival of this man had halted him. He mildly resented the interruption; still, the man appeared to be in some kind of difficulty, and was approaching it by a most devious route. Usher . . . the name meant nothing; uneasily the old priest wondered if he might not be a tax assessor. . . .

Unaware of humiliating speculations, Christopher continued. "You see, from time to time my work has made it necessary for me to study the various religions in the light of their effect upon recent history. It's quite possible, Father, that you may have heard some of my broadcasts."

"Broadcasts?"

"Yes. On the radio. I'm *Christopher* Usher, Father."

"Ah. You must excuse my ignorance, Mr. Usher; while there is a radio in the house, I don't believe I have ever listened to it. Occasionally the curates listen to the baseball games . . . but you spoke of broadcasting upon religious themes: you are a minister?"

"No," said Christopher sharply. "Not a minister." It was incredible; he had never suspected that the otherworldliness of the ordained could extend this far. "I happen to be a news commentator, Father," he explained patiently. "Every night I broadcast to the country upon the trends and events of our times. However, the point I was trying to make is that in all these broadcasts I've never forgotten the religious element. I've never failed to remind my listeners of the tremendous impact of the spiritual upon the lives of all of us."

"Yes, yes, that is all to the good," the priest said, with a vague smile. A broadcaster . . . what *could* the man be driving at? He thought of the sermon, lying unfinished on his desk. He sighed wistfully and said aloud, "Well, then, I must listen to you one evening."

"I hope you will, Father. I think you might enjoy it." Turning from preliminaries, Christopher plunged to the core of the problem. "The point is, Father, I'd like to have a more direct experience of your faith. And not from a professional point of view." He paused, not undrama-

167

tically, before adding, "The fact is, I'm personally interested."

The old priest received the news with an astounding calm. "Ah, I see, I see. You mean you wish to become a Catholic."

"No, no, not at all. That is," Christopher said, "not yet, at any rate. What I have in mind is more of an investigation into your literature at first—"

"So many people," observed the old priest thoughtfully, "are rushing into the arms of the church these days. It is a good thing, of course; the church is universal, it exists for everyone. Yet there are those who fail to understand *why* so many come in. The answer is, of course, that there *is* no single answer; they do so for a variety of reasons. In your own case, however, I should imagine the reason would probably be fairly evident. . . ."

"Well, the whole point is, Father, that I really haven't made any decision to enter—"

"You are growing older," the old priest said. "As you feel age creeping up on you, for the first time you are stirred to contemplate the dismal fact of your own life. You look back, you are filled with the most profound dissatisfaction at what little you have accomplished. And you see that, after all, whatever you *have* managed to achieve in this world, is really not of the slightest importance. Essentially, it is worthless. For once in what has otherwise been a shabby existence, you wish to act to some purpose. . . ."

168

Outraged, Christopher listened to this masterpiece of false interpretation. "Excuse me, Father," he said stiffly, "but that simply isn't at all accurate. It may be true for some people, but certainly not for me. Apart from the fact that I'm still a comparatively young man, I've never quite felt that my work was at all *worthless*. . . ."

"I speak only in the light of ultimate concerns," the old priest said politely.

"Yes, well, the point is that while I don't want to offend you, Father, I haven't any intention of joining your church at the moment. You see, what I really want to do is to make a preliminary inquiry. I thought possibly I might get a list of books by some of your greatest people. Those who were in great difficulty and managed to find solace in their faith."

"You mean you wish me to suggest a program of spiritual reading?"

"More or less, yes. I'd like to keep away from the elementary things as much as I could. I need something I can really, well, really go to work on . . . something by some of your more advanced saints."

"*Advanced* saints . . . ?"

"I'm probably not using the proper terminology, but I'm sure you know what I mean, Father. You see, although I already know quite a bit about the church, as I've said, I'd like to read what the best minds have said on the subject, in their own words. That's why I thought of the saints."

"I see," said the old priest doubtfully. "The ordinary procedure is somewhat different . . . still, if one is accustomed to a more scholarly form of inquiry . . ."

"I think you can trust me on that, Father. All I need is the books."

"I think I have the books," said the priest. "And, if that is what you really want, I shall be happy to lend them to you, of course. Please excuse me for a moment, Mr. Usher."

He left the room and returned shortly with a large bundle, wrapped in newspapers.

"I think these will do very well: Augustine, Aquinas, St. John Chrysostom . . . be particularly careful, if you will, of the Hugh of St. Victor; it is badly bound." Handing them over somewhat hesitantly, he said, "So few people today seem to have the time or the capacity for such studies . . . I hope that you will not find them heavy going."

"I think I'll be able to handle them all right. Thank you very much, Father." Leaving, he said, "And don't worry about the books. I'll get them back to you within a few days."

"A few days," said the old priest, raising his eyebrows. "Well, well, we shall see. . . ."

Shaking his head, he went back to his desk, back to a labor of love. *The liturgy of the Armenians*, he wrote, *is unique among the liturgies of the East in that it is characterized by a single fixed anaphora. The ecclesiastical chant, needless to say, is of the customary enharmonic variety.* . . .

He continued to write, happily and without hesitation. Each Sunday these sermons were attended to with enormous respect, having for his congregation all the fascination of the totally incomprehensible.

At home, Christopher undressed swiftly and went to bed. He switched on the reading light, anticipating, with a sense of odd excitement, the adventure into the unfamiliar realms of the spirit. He tore the wrapper from the bundle and the books fell out, tumbling over the blankets: old volumes, gratifyingly thumbed, reliable highways to the contemplative life. It was only when he opened them, one after another, that he realized, with sinking heart, that here too, consolation was to be denied him. For a fantastic mistake had been made: as a scholar, Christopher was monolingual, and the books before him, with the exception of the St. John Chrysostom (which was in Greek), stood as mute testimony that the universal language of the church was Latin. . . .

eight

ON THE NIGHT BEFORE THE DECISIVE DAY, CHRISTOPHER AND Meredith quarreled. They had, in their married life, quarreled often before, but never so seriously; now, limp from exposure to a week of jeremiad, Meredith had lost her patience, and Christopher, inflamed by the absence of suitable concern along his march toward Armageddon, had lost his self-control.

It was the bad end of a bad week; only that afternoon, Christopher had received in the mail a communication reminding him of the terrors of the abyss. In form, it was nothing more than a listing of names, once passwords in an age of glory, now mere whispers in the memory of man:

1) Tony Wons
2) Frank Crummit
3) Julia Sanderson
4) The A & P Gypsies
5) Graham McNamee
6) Floyd Gibbons

This did not complete the ghostly fellowship; one space remained, on which had been imposed an ominous question mark. The hint was not a veiled one, and Christopher, recalled to fresh thoughts on the subject of oblivion, was shaken to the heels. The cruel *memento mori* was unsigned, but as to its authorship, Christopher had little doubt: it was further evidence of the inhumanity of Adam Flair.

That night, quarrelling with Meredith, he shouted. For professional reasons, even in contention he rarely permitted himself this excess—in the past, it had brought on a mild laryngitis—but tonight caution was in discard. For some time he loudly accused his wife of unfeeling defection.

". . . and the reason you can accept all this with such calm, such apathy, is that you've very probably wanted it to happen all along! It's a terrible thing to have to say, but I actually believe you've been building up an unconscious resentment of my success!"

"Oh, Christopher, really! Unconscious resentment. It's such *cheap* jargon. Like a lay analyst . . ."

". . . although why you should feel that way, so help me God I can't imagine! It isn't as if I'd deserted you

173

along the way. It isn't as if I'd left you behind, kept you in the background. On the contrary. . . ."

"Christopher, if you don't mind I'd just as soon not hear how you've taken me with you to the heights. You've previously expressed yourself on the subject. It's all thoroughly familiar: I've been hitching rides on a superb talent. . ."

"Now there's an excellent example of just what I've been talking about! You say 'superb talent,' but you don't really mean it. . . ."

"Oh, this is all so purposeless!" Rising impatiently from her chair, she said, "I'm going to bed. I just don't want to talk or listen any more."

". . . no, it's really a kind of sneer! But that," he cried triumphantly, "that is where the resentment comes in: in spite of yourself, you're forced to admit that I am a success, that I have reached the top, and the only possible way to account for it is by allowing me talent and plenty of it! Unless, of course," he said, heavily sardonic, "you have some alternative explanation to offer!"

He paused, breathing hard, conscious of victory; at the door, Meredith paused only long enough to hurl a final, swift, pitiless barb.

"Luck," she said briefly. "You are where you are, Christopher, simply because all your adult life you've been so damned unimaginably lucky!"

It struck home, hard, stopping Christopher short; it was a charge he had heard before and one which, above all others, he could not bear. And now, coming from his wife, this treacherous sleight-of-hand which substituted stray winds of chance for the years of conscious, singular achievement . . . it was enough to make him wonder if everyone had gone mad. Going to bed, he slept badly, the spirit of the gibbet coloring his dreams.

He rose earlier than usual, breakfasted, and left the house without a word to anyone. He thought of walking to work; then, because the call from Udolpho might come at any time, he decided to drive. At the studio, he went directly to his office.

"Good morning, Mr. Usher," said his secretary, in some surprise. "You're early today."

Christopher was not in the mood for small talk. "Has Mr. Udolpho called?"

"No, sir, not yet."

"When he does, I'll take it immediately. I'm not in to anyone else for the rest of the day, no matter who it is."

"You have a couple of appointments. Dr. Duquesne has one at eleven-thirty, and a Mr. de Santos of the Bigger Brazil Committee is coming at two."

"Well, cancel them. I can't be bothered with anything like that today." He slammed the door behind him.

Aha, thought the secretary irreverently, mammy's little baby's got the wind up. He reached for the phone, grimacing; the Bigger Brazilian was not a man who took stalling easily.

Inside the office, Christopher sat at his desk, doodling

175

morosely on a green blotting pad. There was work to be done, but he preferred to sit and wait. He waited in this manner for the rest of the morning, but the telephone did not ring.

At home, Meredith was contrite. She sat at late breakfast with the general who, it developed, possessed astonishingly detailed knowledge of the previous night's quarrel.

"I heard everything from my bed," he said simply. "I am by training a light sleeper, my dear, and Christopher's voice seemed to boom through my bedroom walls. And so I could scarcely avoid overhearing." The general smiled comfortingly and reached for the marmalade. "Cheer up, my dear. Let me see a smile on that pretty face. What took place last night was a lovers' spat, nothing more. Believe me, I am a man of some experience in these matters. In the course of my travels the country over, I have stayed with a great many friends, most of them young couples like yourself and Christopher. Without exception, from the time of my arrival they fight bitterly and often. I have known one woman in Savannah, Georgia, otherwise mild and charming to an extreme, to hurl heavy objects at her husband; on one occasion she injured him rather severely. But at bottom, my dear, they are all very much in love with one another, and if you ask me how I know, my answer is that *I can see it in their eyes.* And so it is with you and Christopher: these infrequent minor arguments mean absolutely nothing. Indeed, I often think they are of the greatest benefit: there's nothing quite like a good tiff to clear the air!"

Despite uneasiness, Meredith smiled wanly at the rolling phrases of lunatic cheer. "I'm not sure that we come under your Young Couple classification, General. Besides, it might have been better if I had thrown a heavy object at him. Instead, I did far worse: I called him lucky."

"I heard you," said the general reprovingly. "It is a preposterous charge, as we both so well know. Nothing could be further from the truth. And after a good night's sleep, Christopher will have realized this. Mark my words, my dear, at this very moment he is sitting in his office, recovering his customary good humor. I can see the slow smile breaking over his face as he realizes that last night mountains were made out of molehills!"

"Then he's smiling incommunicado. I tried to telephone him; he won't answer."

"He is ashamed," said the general, spearing a sausage. "Tonight he will come home to you with his arms full of roses."

"I wish I could think so. You see, I'm not at all sorry that I was sharp with him last night; he's been fairly insufferable lately. What does bother me is that I really think I came down too hard, all things considered. . . ."

"Forgive and forget, my dear. Let bygones be bygones. And speaking of tonight, I have a small surprise for you: I have a plan to aid your reconciliation!"

Alarmed, she said, "No, please, General! Please don't—"

"It will be no trouble at all, I assure you. I want to do it. I propose to give a dinner for just the three of us. I know of an excellent restaurant in the city: there will be good food, soft music, just the proper atmosphere for reunion."

"That's very good of you, General, and I appreciate the thought so much. But under the circumstances—"

"Do not think of the inconvenience to me, my dear; there will be none at all. Banish that thought from your mind. I *insist* upon doing it. Let us call it a farewell gift; you see," he said, "I must leave you in a day or so. Possibly even *tomorrow!*"

"Oh . . . ?"

"Things appear to be fairly tense out on the Coast," the general said, in a tone of confidence. "From our point of view, it has become a hornet's nest. They are making a documentary on the California State Guard; apparently the director has proved to be completely intractable. I imagine it will be up to me to pour oil on the troubled waters. Meanwhile, my dear, we will have our little dinner, I will not be denied!"

"There's no necessity for a farewell gift, General, really. We were only too happy—"

"No, no, no, my mind is made up. It will be the best thing in the world for both of you. You will meet tonight in neutral territory: the unfamiliar, delightful setting will do much to relieve any possible strain. An evening on the town is just the thing, believe me!"

"Well . . ." She spoke doubtfully, for it was possible that, for once in a lifetime of unparalleled blunder, the old man had stumbled across the way of wisdom. "It's terribly good of you, General. But I honestly don't know . . . for one thing, there's Christopher. I'm not at all sure that he'd be willing to come."

"Leave Christopher to me. I think I can promise you that he will be more than willing. In fact, my dear, just leave everything to me. Beak Blackburn," he said joyously, "is assuming command. . . ."

Christopher had sent out for his lunch. It was a collation for an invalid: chicken broth, milk, custard. He could not finish it; there had been no call and it was now two o'clock. Grasping at straws, he reflected hopefully on the time differential; in Chicago, it was only one o'clock. An hour could make a difference. There was still time, plenty of time, for the telephone to ring, for the message of cheer, but with the passing of each hour, Christopher grew in despondency. Now flat on his back on the office couch, he stared at the ceiling; his thoughts were oddly diffused, he seemed unable to concentrate; from time to time his stomach muttered like a toy volcano. He thought, in a new and curiously transient way, of others: of how they would be affected by the news of his departure from the air. He thought of those close to him: Lura, Meredith, the five million faceless, nameless devouts who were his audience. He thought of those more remote, less amiable—the figures of misrule to whom the news would come as a blessing: the President, John L. Lewis, Stalin—over this last name he lingered, imagining, without difficulty, the tired, terrible Asiatic face transfixed with sudden glee at the fall of an adversary. From Stalin, he was able to turn without effort to Mr. Bernie Udolpho. At this very moment in Chicago the little financier was devouring another of the immense, oily meals which formed his daily diet. Soon he would finish, would return to his office; *then*, surely, the call would come. Then he would know, one way or the other; until that time he could only wait and continue to think. . . .

In the outer office, the secretary answered the ringing telephone.

"This is General Blackburn speaking. Kindly connect me with Mr. Usher."

"I'm sorry, sir. Mr. Usher is in conference and cannot be disturbed."

"Surely there must be some mistake. This is General *Walter Blackburn* speaking."

"Yes, General. Mr. Usher has been in conference since early this morning. It's quite impossible to say just when he'll be through." The secretary was a young man not without whimsy; seized by a happy inspiration, he added: "He's with several men from the Pentagon."

"The Pentagon. Oh. I see. Yes. Yes, yes. Well, in that event, of course, we must not disturb him." The general seemed oddly distracted. "By no means. No no. First things first. It's quite all right."

"Shall I tell him you'll call again, General?"

"No no. Under no circumstances. That is to say, I think not." After a moment, he added, "You might, however, give Mr. Usher a message for me. Privately, you understand: when he is *quite free.* . . ."

"Yes, General."

"Ask him if he will kindly meet me this evening immediately following his broadcast. It is a matter of the most vital importance. I shall be," said the general, "at the Club Ga-Ga."

"Very well, General. I'll tell him."

Later, when he went into Christopher's office with a batch of late news dispatches, and added them to the untouched pile on the table, he said, "General Blackburn telephoned. He seemed to want to talk to you pretty badly."

"You know what I told you. I'm in to no one but Mr. Udolpho."

"I explained that you weren't available, so he left a message."

"Well, tear it up. I don't want it. . . ."

The general said: "Everything is arranged, my dear. As I predicted it would be."

"Really? General, I *have* underestimated you, grievously. You're really quite wonderful." Impulsively, she planted a kiss on the fine old forehead; the general received it, beaming. "How did you do it? What did you say? Was Christopher still angry? Had he heard from Udolpho?"

"Now, now, my dear, do not press me for details. I never reveal my secrets. Christopher himself will tell you everything tonight; that is how it should be. He is to meet us directly after his broadcast. I have taken care of everything; your only concern, my dear, is to look your radiant best. . . ."

The end of the afternoon, and Christopher, back at his desk, poked dully through accumulated news. For the first time he felt the relative meaninglessness of global events; the truth came to him with melancholy irony. Here, before him, was a totality of information, funneled to him post-haste from every corner of the world, however remote, however obscure, yet the single piece of intelligence that mattered, that had any relevance to the moment, remained unavailable to him, locked in the uncommunicative heart of a Chicago millionaire. For there had been no word, no word either way, and in the waning hours of the long and fruitless afternoon, Christopher, certain now that the feared possibility had at last come to pass, spoke aloud, summing up disaster in a succinct and solemn phrase.

"*They'll never hear me again!*" he said.

Strictly speaking, this was not quite true: his listeners would continue to hear him nightly until the expiration of his present contract. Yet in the larger sense it was true: from this moment on his days with them were numbered. Two weeks, perhaps three, and then—the void. He knew instinctively—and no man trusted his instincts more—that the silent telephone spelled defeat; the uttered acknowledgment of this as fact left him strangely purged of bitterness. Toward those responsible, he felt a commendable if rather eerie absence of ill will; somewhat to his surprise, he was conscious only of a vague, engulfing emotion which he could describe only as sadness. It was not a sadness for himself; it was a sadness for others: a curious, universal pity, broad enough for all, but concentrated chiefly on those five million souls for whom the deprivation would be most severe.

"Poor devils," he muttered, and pulled his typewriter toward him. The deadline of the broadcast hour approached, and now he was ready, for in the past few minutes the skeleton of tonight's instruction had begun to take shape, its pale bones looming through the mists of compassion. He knew exactly what was demanded of him. He pushed all news dispatches to one side; in what he had to say tonight, the ephemeral would have small place. Occasionally, in the past, he had done a broadcast somewhat similar in kind, in which, the customary keen analysis of the topical abandoned for the evening, he had spoken *sub specie aeternitatis*.

For such a broadcast it was his custom to select as his subjects great figures from the American past: Lincoln,

Teddy Roosevelt, Salmon P. Chase, General Custer. In each there was a lesson; around each he wove the bitter-sweet recollections of preautomotive days when men were strong, competition was free, and the chestnut tree bloomed undefiled. They were leisurely, reflective essays; they provided a valuable change of pace when news was scarce, or when he felt it necessary to remind his listeners of blessings irrevocably lost.

Tonight, there would be just such a broadcast. It would be slightly more contemporary than most; it would also be more personal, for the subject he had chosen was that of himself. He would review, quietly, nostalgically, his nine years of broadcast leadership; together, he and his listeners would re-examine the great moments of their lives together. In no sense of the word would it be a swan song (the actual farewell would be made later, more formally); it would be a warning, a muted hint that he could not be with them always, a cushion against the shock to come. Gently fingering the keyboard of his typewriter, he began the marshaling of memory; under his fingers the sentences shaped themselves, slowly at first, then with a startling rapidity. It came very close to being automatic writing; indeed, he could not recall a time when his words had seemed to spring so directly and unaided from the human heart. . . .

". . . from Europe, from Asia, from Africa, from our own country, every moment of every day points to the fact that we're moving swiftly, marching on, going great guns and faster than ever before. Well, there are those who say it's a good thing. They say it's all for the best in a bigger and a better world. Maybe they're right. But sometimes I wonder. Sometimes I wonder whether we—and that goes for all of us—aren't moving just a bit *too* quickly. Sometimes I wonder if we all wouldn't be better off if someone in a responsible position stood up and said: 'Wait a minute. Wait just one minute. Stop the music. Speed is all very well, but let's all remember that Rome wasn't built in a day, that in the famous fable of our childhood days, it wasn't the hare who won the race!' Yes, sometimes I wonder if that wouldn't be a good thing. Sometimes as I sit here before the microphone, I wonder whether it wouldn't be a good thing to call a halt on all the spending, the pump-priming, the happy-go-lucky, spend-what-you-want, we'll-pay-the-bills diplomacy that seems to be the chief export from Washington these days. And I don't know but that some of you might agree with me. I don't know but that some of you who've been listening to these broadcasts for the past nine years might not just possibly be nodding your heads and saying, "Usher may be right. He's been right in the past. . . ."

He recalled, as he typed, all the times he *had* been right in the past. And to think that in a few short weeks, such a record would count for nothing, would not even be *remembered* . . . it was heartbreaking, and he could only sigh and continue typing, even more rapidly than before, reminding his audience of past comforts afforded by one man with vision:

". . . recall those dark days of 1943, I said: 'Take heart, America! Stalingrad could be important. If Hitler fails there, it could mean much. If Russia can hold, can advance, it might be a different story. If. . . .' "

Similar apocalyptic disclosures came readily to mind. . . .

The façade of the Club Ga-Ga was a rainbow of dancing neon; there was a giant doorman with a battered face and a military greatcoat which was lime in color with canary epaulets.

Inside, Meredith found herself in tropical surroundings. No detail of flora or fauna had been spared to provide authenticity: palm trees adorned the room in lavish arrangement, sprouting from semiconcealed pots; impressive greenery twirled and twined overhead and on the sides of the room, penetrating crevices in the walls of split bamboo. Through the dripping fronds of palm there were glimpses of coconuts and occasional stuffed monkeys, the latter gazing sightlessly ahead with disconsolate eyes of glass. On a raised platform a small orchestra played animated Latin melodies on assorted skins, strings and gourds; the entire room was excessively crowded and unbelievably noisy.

Here the general was not without friends. . . .

The hat-check girl said, "Hiya, honey. Long time no see."

"Good evening, Titania."

"What about it, honey: we gonna have another war?"

"I doubt it very seriously, Titania; all the signs are against it. Although a few months spent in uniform would be just the thing for that young man of yours."

The girl laughed coarsely. "That's what you think," she said.

The general murmured to Meredith, "The people here are very simple and natural; very like the peasantry of some of the European countries. Do you like the place, my dear?"

"Yes . . ." She looked dubiously about this setting for the proposed reconciliation. "It's a bit . . . unusual, isn't it?"

"It has swank," the general said comfortably. "Swank and atmosphere. Without these, my dear, no club can hope to survive. The Club Ga-Ga, I am happy to say, is doing famously. It is an old favorite of mine. Ah, good evening, Dino."

"Hello, General. Good to see you again." A short, pale man with inky eyes and smiling lips, he led them to a table at the edge of the tiny dance floor.

"Good evening, Ernest. Good evening, Paul. Ah, Anya . . ."

Meredith said: "You seem to know a great many people."

"Yes, yes. You see, my dear, my duties during the war years were secret and extensive; they obliged me to fre-

187

quent places such as this in the interest of our national security. Years ago, such would not have been the soldier's lot; however, we must remember," he said happily, "that the last war was a *total* war!"

Meredith looked at her watch. "I can't help wondering about Christopher. Shouldn't he be here by now?"

"It's much too soon, my dear. You must allow him time to change, to freshen up after his broadcast. Naturally, he will want to look his best for the occasion. Never fear, he will be here. . . ."

Up on the bandstand, the leader had turned to wave at the general. "Allo, allo," he cried.

"Hello, Pepi," the general called back. Lowering his voice, he said, "Pepi, my dear, is one of the very few men in the country today who properly interpret the samba. Do you dance it, by the way? No? I will teach you; it will be a great surprise for Christopher. . . ."

The broadcast was over. Although it had been autobiographical, it had not been extravagantly so; Christopher had felt no need to pad his part in history. He had stuck to the facts; he had told the simple, straightforward story of a man whose country owed him far more than it could ever hope to pay. Now back in his office, he settled down beside the telephone to wait; although confident that sentence had been passed, there remained the traditional hope of the condemned for reprieve.

He waited for more than an hour. The waiting was

tedious; restless, he sought diversion in the pursuit of the unfamiliar: he began to read. On his desk were a number of books, submitted by publishers, naïve men, hopeful of broadcast mention of their products. In the grip of boredom, Christopher picked up one of these and opened it aimlessly:

. . . have seen how Western Europe first achieved cultural unity in the Carolingian period. Yet within the limits of the Carolingian World itself there was an almost immeasurable gap between the artificial humanism of men like Servatus Lupus and Walafrid Strabo and the mentality of the warrior noble or the peasant serf. . . .

It was precisely this sort of thing, this impractical preoccupation with the historical backdrop, which had proved so useless to him in the past; it could not hope to hold him now. He passed from books to reading which promised greater reward: there were advertising brochures from the office of Jason Rooney. One of these offered vivid evidence that Mr. Bernie Udolpho, a farsighted man, was keeping up with the world:

. . . from the laboratories of Agrarian Products comes still another revolutionary, all-vegetable analgesic: the new improved UNGUENTOMIC! Not a liquid, not a jelly, not a salve, UN-GUENTOMIC is a balm . . . UNGUENTOMIC IS THE ATOM-BALM! Scientifically tested, approved by leading physicians everywhere, UNGUENTOMIC is the new miracle balm guaranteed to offer you welcome relief from flash burns due to atomic explosion! This will be especially welcome news to all you folks in the big cities along our eastern seaboard. Of course we all hope that the atom bomb will never be dropped. But if one should be dropped, you'll want to be able to reach for that tube of UNGUENTOMIC in a hurry! Simply rub it on the affected part, and presto! you'll feel blessed relief. A word of caution: UNGUENTOMIC is not designed to protect against the effects of radiation. It's strictly for burns. So remember the name: It's UNGUENTOMIC . . . it's the ATOM-BALM!

Christopher pushed it aside dispiritedly; as a piece of copy it had everything—ingenuity, vision, timing, *smash* —yet he was not in the mood to appreciate it. His mood, indeed, had remained constant for several hours. It was negative: there was this curiously neutral, dismal benevolence, nothing more. He seemed not to care. He was not angry with anyone; he had simply lost hope. He had lost his buoyant outlook. Like a man who, in his middle years, suddenly loses the faith of his fathers, Christopher had lost, instead, all capacity for optimism. The silver lining might still be there; he no longer believed in it. He was not of that proud oligarchy who hold themselves sole guardians of wisdom; less selfish, he wished only to communicate, to share, to instruct others less well-informed than himself. But now the pipe lines had been closed. As wise, as knowledgeable as he had ever been, he was faced with the tragic question: *who was now to know this?* Denied access to his audience, he would be alone with his thoughts. Like some great bear in hibernation, he would be forced to devour his own substance, to feast unassisted on the food of his accumulated wisdom. It was a rich banquet, far too rich for one alone, and yet with whom could be share? Direct communication was possible with few. There was always Lura, but at the thought of her as his principal auditor, he could not help frowning. Superb in her way, there was no denying that she was not at home in the climate of the intellect. In her cultural experience there had been astounding lacunae, of which he had of late become increasingly aware—there had been terrible, vacant, uncomprehending seconds of silence which had followed some of his most striking observations—and which, under the circumstances, he could not but deplore. There was, then, Meredith—at the name, he winced, recalling the previous evening and her calculated cruelty toward him. *Lucky!* Yet now, in his rather extraordinary mood, he was not resentful; he even felt a disposition toward forgiveness. She had been cruel to him, yes, but there had been times when she had not. They had, after all, been long together: alone of all his acquaintances, she was capable of understanding him at his best. In the waning moments, as the telephone refused to ring, and as he became increasingly conscious of his own aloneness, sentimentality welled up within him like a geyser: his eyes moistened, and he thought of his wife with tenderness, affection. It was even possible that in some unknown way, he had prodded her to the offense; impulsively, he decided to go home, to forgive, and, if absolutely necessary, to be forgiven.

He waited a few minutes more; then, as the telephone continued its silence, he left the building and went home. . . .

"Meredith!" he called. "Meredith!" Dramatic instinct

told him to add the words: "I'm home!" It made no difference; he was answered only by his own echo.

The maid came trotting up from below. "Mrs. Usher's gone out to dinner, Mr. Usher."

"Out to dinner? When? Where? With Mrs. Branch?"

"She went out about a couple of hours ago. With the general. She didn't say where."

Blackness returned. Willing to do his part, to do far more than his part, he had been met again by another desertion: his wife had chosen his darkest hour to go dining with a stupefying old man! It was too much; in anger and despair, he sped to the one corner where welcome was assured. . . .

"You know what you need, Chris baby?" Lura said, after a while. "You need a drinkie-winkie. Just a *little* one."

"No, no, I never touch it." It was true; when he had first gone on the air, prudence had dictated the way of total abstention. He knew that it was but a short step from the friendly drink to the fuddled reason, the thick speech, the incautious remark; along such a road had broadcasters perished.

"Well, neither do *I*. But sometimes, Chris baby, when you're not here, Lura gets *lonely*. And if she has just a wee drinkie-winkie, she feels *lots* better. Try it, Chris baby; it's like *medicine*. Look." From somewhere in the cabinet of the television set, she produced temptation.

"*Pinch-bottle*," she said, in tones of awe. "Brother

brought it to me for a present. Have just a *little* one, Chris baby. You'll feel so good."

"Well. . . ." After all, he thought sadly, why not? The reason for abstinence no longer existed; soon, soon he would be off the air. And surely, on this glum night, he was entitled to what few pleasures remained for him. "Perhaps a small one," he said. "A very small one. Will you have one too, Lura?"

"Mmmm, just a *little* one. . . ."

As a dancer, the general was tireless. . . .

"The important thing is the rhythm, my dear: boom ba boom, boom ba boom ba ba—ah that's better, much better. . . ."

They continued to whirl, the center of all eyes. The general was flushed and in the highest possible spirits; Meredith was in a state of near exhaustion.

"General, let's sit down for just a moment. What could have happened to Christopher?"

"Nothing at all, my dear. He will be here presently; the night is young."

"But it really is quite late. Couldn't you phone the studio, just to make sure?"

"Very well, my dear, if it will ease your mind." Somewhat grudgingly the general left the dance floor in search of a telephone. He returned almost immediately.

"At the broadcasting station they say he left some time

ago; I think we may expect to see him at any moment. Meanwhile, shall we have another turn or two . . . ?"

Christopher had had more than one small drink. He had had several, all of them rather large. It had been an enriching experience; he felt wonderful, he felt alive, he felt young, he felt ready for action—action of any description. He strode around the room with long uncertain steps, talking rapidly and incoherently, spilling drinks on the rug as he walked.

"Let's go stepping," he announced suddenly. He looked at Lura with preternaturally bright eyes. "Go out and go stepping. Hell with people. Caution to the winds. Christopher Usher, that's who!" Turning sharply, he glared at imaginary bystanders.

"Party-party? Oh yes, Chris baby! I'll have to change; I'll be just a second. . . ."

Left alone, Christopher began to sing. He sang popular tunes of twenty years before; he remembered them imperfectly and sang them badly. In between the snatches of song, he mumbled random thoughts on a subject close to his heart.

"Christopher Usher," he said. "*In person*. One man they don't push around. Nobody. Hell of a smart apple. The best, *the very damn best*. Let's go stepping. . . ."

Lura emerged, dewy-eyed and glossy.

"Come on," she cried. "Come on, Chris baby!"

Christopher did a facetious little dance step. "Paint town red," he said, nodding.

In the taxi, Lura said, "I know a *wonderful* place to go," and gave directions. Christopher settled back against the cushions with a sigh. Quite unexpectedly, there had been a swift ebbing of elation; he felt odd, not quite healthy. With the passing of gaiety, he felt once more the overwhelming sorrow for himself, and he began to talk rapidly and confusedly, not of triumph, but of adversity. Lura listened, at first uncomprehending, then suddenly alert.

"What was that, Chris baby?" she asked, her forehead wrinkling slightly. "Tell Lura that again."

He did; the wrinkles deepened.

"You mean you're all *through?*"

Christopher nodded. "Dead duck. Washed up. Ask Flair. Crucified, by God. One of finest living Americans, crucified." So deeply did he feel that he began to weep.

"Don't cry, Chris baby. Be sensible. Listen to Lura. You mean you're *ruined?* No more broadcasts, *ever?* Tell Lura: it's *important* to her!"

Christopher slumped lower in his seat; he belched slightly. "Feel awful," he moaned.

Lura sat erect, staring thoughtfully ahead. It was not an easy world, there were always decisions to be made . . . beside her, a tear fell on the back of her hand, a reminder that once again the dogs had found the scent, that still another honeymoon was nearing its end. . . .

The cab stopped; Christopher dismounted with difficulty. "Where?" he asked, staring foggily around. "Got a right to know. *Christopher Usher!*"

"Ssshh," she said. Still thoughtfully, she pushed him in the direction of the gaily-colored entrance; he began to run, erratically, carried along by the momentum of the push, dragging her after him.

"Chris, be *careful!*" she cried, suddenly alarmed, but she was too late; already they were careening, hopelessly off balance, through the open door. . . .

Inside, they fell in a great crash. Lura fell over him and lay sprawled across his lap; people crowded around; he looked up dazedly, conscious only of the great jumble of faces. Then, suddenly, the fog parted, and miraculously sobered, he saw, against the wall of anonymous flesh, the horrified face of his wife. And above the din, he heard, crystal-clear, a familiar, fruity voice, proclaiming like a death knell:

"Why bless my soul, it's *Christopher* . . . !"

nine

CHRISTOPHER AWAKENED TO THE WORST MORNING IN HIS memory. He was in extreme physical misery: his head was heavy and ridden with the sharpest pains; his eyes ached; he was seized with spasms of nausea. Opening his eyes to the blinding light of the morning, he saw that his bedroom was in a state of unprecedented disorder: his trousers had been flung, negligent of creases, across the radio; his shirt was on the floor, beneath his shoes; chairs had been overturned and lay sidelong on the rug, like the forlorn wreckage of battle.

"My God," he groaned; mystified, he wondered if there had been burglars, if he had been the victim of felonious assault. After a moment he sat up, torment streaking through his head; he put one foot over the edge of the bed. A bottle of ink, upset long hours before, had dribbled steadily throughout the night onto the floor; it was into this thin blue pool that Christopher now stepped. The moist discomfort revealed to him for the first time that he had gone to bed with his socks on and that these, indeed, constituted his entire sleeping costume.

"What's *happened?*" he muttered, and then, slowly, agonizingly, he began to remember. Not for him the merciful blackout of the morning after; step by step the night passed before his eyes in mortifying review, complete to the last shameful detail. He saw Lura . . . pinch-bottle . . . palm trees . . . *Meredith!* He shook his head and shuddered.

To wash, to dress, to descend stairs was torture; nevertheless, he accomplished all, physical wretchedness paling before his dread of the meeting to come. As he went uneasily down the long staircase, he began to repeat to himself, over and over again, a question that had not occurred to him since childhood: *what will I say . . . ?*

There was no one in the dining room; he rang for the maid.

"Has Mrs. Usher been down to breakfast yet?"

"No sir." He thought she looked queerly at him. "The general was down, Mr. Usher, and then he went. He left a letter for you." She pointed to the letter on his plate, then turned and fled back to the uncomplicated world of the basement kitchen.

After a moment Christopher opened the envelope. The note was one of cheery farewell:

My dear Christopher,

May an old soldier dare to hope that this note will serve as some expression of appreciation for your superb hospitality? Unfortunately, I must leave you this morning, my dear fellow; I am off to the wars once more. I am distressed that a more personal farewell is not possible, but I must leave at the crack of dawn—the army, as we both so well know, is no respecter of persons!—and I assumed that, under the circumstances, you would not care to be disturbed.

I shall, of course, continue to look forward to your broadcasts on my travels. They are magnificent, Christopher; I sometimes wonder if you realize just how good they really are. I confidently predict that in five years time the entire world will come to recognize in you the Voice of Sanity in a Troubled Age. You will grow with the years, Christopher; there is not a doubt of it!

By the bye, your wife is staying at her father's house for the time being. She appeared to be quite upset at the events of last evening. I comforted her as best I could, but the poor girl seemed actually distraught. She spoke rather wildly about leaving you, and other nonsense of that sort. I firmly believe, however, that all was spoken in the anger of the moment, and I know that in the sober light of day all this will seem laughable to both of you.

Again, my dear fellow, my most sincere appreciation. I shall look forward eagerly to my next visit with you, when I hope I shall be able to make it a real stay. Until then, rest assured that whatever may come, I shall be listening. . . .

Christopher could eat nothing. After a while, he drove over to his father-in-law's house. As yet he had been unable to devise a suitable pattern of approach; it would have to depend, he thought, upon his reception by Meredith. Uncomfortably, he speculated upon the nature of that reception; one by one, the alternatives suggested themselves. She could be angry, unforgiving, vulnerable only to abject apology; it would be humiliating, but he would offer it. Or—and this was at once distressing and yet, somehow more congenial—she could be weeping, hurt, but willing to forgive. Or—and there was just this possibility—she might not see him at all. It was unlikely, but barely possible. . . .

None of these surmises was accurate. Meredith came down to meet him within a few minutes of his arrival; her appearance was encouraging. She seemed calm, in possession of herself, and if she were not overly friendly, at least she was not hostile.

"Good morning, Christopher."

"Good morning," he said, and smiled tentatively; untutored in the protocol for the wayward husband, he nevertheless felt that it was up to him to keep things going. He began to talk rapidly. "Although as a matter of fact, it's not a good morning. Not for me, at any rate; I've never felt worse in my life. I know I don't look well, Meredith. I know that. As a matter of fact, I haven't even eaten breakfast yet. . . ."

"No breakfast? Your dark friend can't cook?"

It was a nasty, a perilous, an unfair turn; he said, "Now look, Meredith. Please. Listen to me for just a minute. I know what you must be thinking; I don't blame you. But I'd like you to listen to what I have to say. The whole point is that I'd like you to hear my side of the story before you pass judgment. I'd like—"

"You'd like me to understand."

"Well, yes. Yes, I would, Meredith. I would very much." Pleased by the ready comprehension, he hurried on; a possible out had suggested itself to him. "You see, I know I'm at fault. But it isn't as bad as you think, Meredith. Not by a long shot. You probably think that this is something that's been going on for some time. But what I'd like to explain to you is the real truth. And I'd like you to realize that we're both—"

"We're both adults," she said quietly. "We're not a couple of children. Is that it, Christopher?"

"In a manner of speaking, I suppose it is. Although not exactly." He regarded her suspiciously; the words had an ominous undertone. He realized, suddenly, that she was not really co-operating at all. "Damn it, Meredith!" he said loudly. "We ought to be able to discuss this, to talk it out. After all, we are married. . . ."

"A thought that is always uppermost in your mind, I'm sure. Christopher, I simply am not going to fence with you. The truth is that I don't want to hear what you have to say. I don't want to hear any more from you or about you at all. And don't ask me to be reasonable. I don't feel like being particularly reasonable. And above all, I

don't feel like discussing this matter with you, now or
at any other time. . . ."

At this moment, Christopher was endowed with a rare
prescience; with sinking heart, he said: "You're thinking
of leaving . . ."

"I've already left, Christopher; you didn't give me a
great variety of choice. I'm going to live here for the time
being; I'll send for what things I need later in the week;
I won't require any money or assistance of any kind from
you. I think that's all I have to say."

"Divorce. . . ."

"Ultimately, I suppose. I haven't been thinking too
much about details. In any event, whatever is done will
be done quietly. There'll be no scandal before your public,
Christopher; that should relieve your mind." She walked
quickly away from him, toward the hall. "I really don't
want to talk about it any more," she said.

"Wait!" he ran around in front of her, barring the
doorway; his hands were thrown out at his sides in a
gesture of helpless entreaty. "Wait a minute, Meredith.
I can explain all this. I want you to realize what you're
doing; my God we've been married for twenty-one years!
Think of that, Meredith! Think of yourself, think," he
said, "think of me. I need you. . . ."

"Yes," she said slowly. "Yes, I know you do. The
trouble is that you need other things more. You need five
million listeners every day, you need your little girl friend.
I could take the five million listeners, even take the fact

that I had become one of them. What I could never take, I'm afraid, is the girl friend. You see, I was unprepared, Christopher: I didn't expect her."

"Listen," he said desperately. "Listen, Meredith: I'll tell you something you don't know. I'm through! Udolpho canceled. He did it in the worst possible way: he didn't even bother to call. Don't you see what that means?"

The bid for pity was not entirely successful.

"It means that you'll need the creature comforts more than ever. I'm sure you know someone who can provide you with them. Good-by, Christopher."

Swiftly, she left him. He stood staring up the stairs after her, feeling vacant, ill, uncertain of having made his point. There had been a terrible coldness that he had never before seen, an unwillingness to listen to reason, a frightening disregard for the broken home, his future. . . . He was plagued by the fear that possibly she meant what she said. . . .

He went home and sat in the library, brooding. There was a way, there had to be a way, of explanation . . . after some time, he telephoned to his father-in-law's office.

"Dr. Wrenn? This is Christopher calling . . ."

"Ah. The sportsman. . . ."

The dry old voice was detached, infinitely remote, not quite of this world; often, in his relationship with the old man, Christopher had wondered whether he had not long ago drifted into the muzzy clime of senility.

"Doctor," he said, speaking slowly and with great distinctness, "as you know, I've always hesitated to intrude my family affairs on my in-laws. The point is, however, that now I'm afraid I'm going to have to ask a favor of you."

"A favor? I am in a position to do few favors. I am not a man of influence; I am a physician. . . ."

Christopher swore briefly to himself. "Listen, Doctor, it's not that kind of favor. This is extremely personal. I want you, if you'll be good enough, to talk to Meredith for me. I don't know what to do about her."

"Meredith? Is something wrong with Meredith?"

"*She's left me,* Doctor. You must have known that; she's staying at your house."

"Ah. Yes, I knew *that.* But you seemed to imply that something was wrong . . . ?"

"*That's* what's wrong," Christopher said, in some exasperation. "Look, Doctor, this is extremely serious; I wonder if you could give it your undivided attention. Now, I imagine Meredith told you what happened last night?"

"She mentioned something; it was all very vague. As I remember it, you had been in this public place with some woman, brawling . . ."

"Not brawling, Doctor. Not brawling at all. And actually, the whole thing sounds much worse than it was." Quickly, he told a story of humiliation, a story which, however, was less humiliating than it might have been, for Christopher had decided to make the slight alterations necessary for the preservation of his family, himself. Lura, then, in the telling became a casual, encountered for the first time that night by a man far gone in drink; she had clung to him, led him, and he, insentient, had followed. . . .

". . . and that's all there was to it, Doctor. I admit that it's enough. I admit that it was foolish, stupid for a man of my years and experience to get into that condition. I fully admit that. But the point is that Meredith appears to think it was much more than that; she apparently seems to feel that this woman was more than, well, just a chance meeting. And I can't talk to her at all, I can't explain the facts. That's why I thought that perhaps you. . . ."

"You feel that if she could get the truth her thinking might be changed?"

"I'm sure of it, yes."

"And you wish me to be the one to get this truth to her, so to speak?"

"Yes, yes, that's it exactly." Christopher was encouraged: conversation with this old man was a maddening series of ups and downs, but now it seemed to be definitely up. "You see, all you have to do is to convince her that it isn't at all what she suspects and I'm sure she'll return where she belongs."

"Yes. Of course I have long made it a practice never to interfere in my daughter's marriage. . . ."

"But don't you see that this wouldn't be interference at all? I'm *asking* you to do it!"

"And yet," continued the doctor imperturbably, "there

was one occasion on which I did interfere, one exception to my rule. It is this exception about which I should like to tell you now; I think you might find it interesting. . . ."

Oh my God, Christopher thought irritably, never mind the history, come on, come on. . . .

"It began, I should say, about one month ago. At that time, a certain man, for whom I had never cared greatly, suddenly began to trouble me. Or rather, he did not trouble me; his actions did. I noticed that for some time he had been keeping long and irregular hours, departing from his home at all hours of the night on mysterious errands, and for these odd actions he gave the excuse of his work. Now, I am not a suspicious man, but neither am I a fool; moreover, I had the advantage of not being blinded by affection. So I did something which I had heretofore never dreamed of doing: I hired, for the purposes of inquiry, a private detective. I did this only because the happiness of someone very dear to me was involved. Did you say something?"

There had been the sound of sharp exclamation at the other end.

"To continue," said the doctor, after a pause. "I cannot in honesty say that I liked this detective. He drank, he was dirty, and I suspected him of dishonesty; nevertheless, professionally he was competent. He did his work well. For more than three weeks he observed this man of mystery who had suddenly found it necessary to labor so hard; as a result of this observation, I was given a full set of completely detailed reports. I will not bore you with their contents. It is sufficient to say that they were sordid in the extreme; taken together they told the story of a cheap woman and an infinitely cheaper man. I did not show these reports to the man's wife at the time. Quite foolishly, I hoped that in some manner matters could be improved, that somehow there might be a turn for the better. And so I kept the evidence to myself. That is, I kept it to myself," he said, "until last night. Then, to use a phrase of your own, the necessity arose for 'explaining the facts.' I can assure you that she now has a fair appreciation of the situation. Are you still listening, by the way . . . ?"

In the library of Christopher's home, the telephone receiver lay on the desk; the thin, almost inaudible words coming from it ceased, giving way to a faint mechanical buzz. Christopher sat with his head in his hands. In the dreadful, dry old voice, he had come to experience for the first time the limitless contempt of another; in the urbanely whispered words, he had heard the sentence of doom, irrevocably pronounced. . . .

Later in the day, he went back to Lura. He went without enthusiasm, almost without volition; an unhappy traveler, against whom all frontiers had closed, he made his way instinctively to the one unalien land.

Here too, dark forces lurked. . . .

"Chris!" The greeting contained astonishment, rather than delight; Lura said: "I didn't expect you so soon. . . ."

"No," he said, looking about him. "So I see." The room was in a turmoil: airplane luggage, half-packed, lay open on the floor; dresses, hats, stockings, a mountain of lingerie, torn from hangers and drawers, had been thrown hastily across the divan; beside the luggage was a pile containing shoes, cruets of scent, and a few of the more portable possessions of the hotel.

"You're packing," he said superfluously. "What's happening here, anyway?"

"Chris baby, this makes me so sad. I mean, you'll have to understand how I *feel*. . . ."

The bathroom door opened suddenly and a small, swarthy man stepped gaily into the room; it was the man whom Christopher had seen with Lura on the street. At the sight of Christopher he halted and looked uneasily at Lura; then he smiled furtively at Christopher.

"Aha," he said. "How are you, good sir?"

Christopher ignored him. "Is your brother the one responsible for all this?" he asked Lura.

The swarthy man snickered unexpectedly; dark eyebrows rose and fluttered in amused appreciation. "*Brother!*" he echoed. "Oh, my good sir, how rich!"

"Chris baby," Lura said, after a pause, "Lura told you a little fib. He's not really my *brother*—"

"He is instead her husband!" cried the swarthy man, with a theatrical flourish of his hands. "Bubu Andriescu is here!"

"We're going to be married all over again, Chris. You see I couldn't tell you *that*. You might have been *hurt*. . . ."

Christopher continued to stare at her. "I see," he said, in a strained voice. "I see how it is. You've been having a grand time for yourself, haven't you? A grand time at my expense. And all the while you've had this little rat sneaking around. . . ." He moved threateningly toward the swarthy man, who skipped to the rear of Lura with some agility.

"Have a care, good sir!" he cried. "I am not unarmed!" In support of his words he produced a small silver revolver which he held in a dangerously unsteady hand. "Do not come nearer!" he warned. "I will be within my rights: you are coming between a wife and her husband. Marriage is sacred: I know the American laws!"

Lura spoke soothingly, rationally. "You've been a wonderful *friend*, Chris baby, but Bubu was my *husband*, after all. He just came back last week. From *Rumania*. We're going to be married and go back to Hollywood, back," she said, "to my *career*."

"The sacredness of the home," reminded the swarthy man nervously. "The law is very severe."

"Chris baby, Lura wants you to *understand*. After all, she has to think of herself a *little* bit, doesn't she?" Closing her eyes, she slumped into the familiar thespic crouch. "I'm happy-happy now, Chris baby. Lura's the happiest little girl in the world," she sighed. "But she'll never *never* forget her Chris baby. . . ."

The sound of the slamming door informed her that once more she had failed to captivate an audience; Chris baby had gone. . . .

And so, at last, he was alone. . . .

In his office, he sat at his desk, close to panic at the thought. He shut his eyes as once again the ache of memory began to throb insistently: one month, two weeks, ago, he had had a wife, Lura, a vast radio family. Now, all were gone. He wondered how much a man could be expected to bear, at exactly what point of strain the bones of the spirit, bending, began to crack. Physically he was in bad shape, the worst shape in years. Frequent glances at the mirror showed him what the triple loss, plus the unfamiliar dissipations of the night before, could do to the most robust countenance. He felt tired, beaten, old; for two mornings now, he had not exercised.

So undeservedly alone! It was an impossibility, an incredible fact which every thought, every physical movement brought him with a solid, dull pain. He could not raise his eyes in the office without encountering some memento of pleasures once enjoyed, now lost forever. There was one—just one—souvenir of Lura: it was half of a bonbon. . . .

"Mmmm!" she had said, white teeth dividing the candy in two. "Half for me, and half for you, Chris baby. We'll always keep them . . . like a *pledge*. . . ."

It had been simple, infinitely touching; now the pledge

210

was on his desk: a cracked and graying glucose reminder of deprivation and betrayal. . . .

There was a photograph of Meredith. It had been taken when she was some years younger, at the time, in fact, when he had decided to leap from the sports page into the World. Then, with soft, supporting words, she had borne him in his flight:

"If it's what you really want to do, Christopher, if you're so unhappy on the paper, then of course I'm for it. It's something new, of course, but they seem to feel you can do it. And so do I. . . ."

The faith, the love of years ago. . . .

And all around, on everyside, wherever he looked, there were the visible, poignant reminders of professional triumphs, of years of leadership. There were citations from the Treasury Department, the Red Cross, the SPCA; there were jade figurines from a grateful China; there were framed honorary degrees; there were trophies, awards, an ill-tempered letter from Henry Wallace; there were *photographs*: he was hanging Mussolini in effigy (it had been the high-water mark of a wonderful week in Arkansas); he was shaking hands with Eduard Beneš; he was posed with Eddie Rickenbacker, signing a short-snorter; he was sitting with Berney Baruch on a park bench—and in the picture, *Baruch was listening*. . . .

"My God!" he moaned. "O my God!"

On his desk was a sample letter from the morning mail; automatically his eyes fell on it. . . .

Dear Mr. Usher:

Is there a Pulitzer prize for radio broadcasters? After hearing your marvelous talk of last night, my sister and I are convinced that there is no one in the country who deserves it more than you. We listen to you every night and have done so for years and years. . . .

"O MY GOD!" he groaned; it was too much, too much . . .

And still there remained the question, unanswered, indeed, scarcely asked: *what to do now?* He would miss Lura, he would miss Meredith; it was only human. And he would miss five million people, listening, listening . . . while he, silent, would have so much to tell them! He wondered if in some way he could not continue on the radio; he doubted it. He wondered what else could possibly offer itself, and in partial reply, the mocking words of Adam Flair came floating back to him:

". . . presumably you've maintained cordial contact with your former associates on the sports page; you could go back there. . . ."

But could he? Could he, now alone, embark on retrogression? Could he, too, go back to the managing editor, back to the sly, ill-averted smiles with which his former associates were accustomed to greet the failure of those who had thought to rise above them. Or, most important of all, after an approximate decade spent in the company of the great and in the guidance of so many, could he now return to clubhouse interviews with *jockeys?* It was unthinkable, and yet, in this moment of triple crisis, it was the thought which dominated his mind. . . .

The telephone rang and continued to ring; finally, wearily, Christopher answered.

"Yes, yes. . . ."

"Usher?" asked a familiar voice. "Udolpho."

It made no sense. . . .

"Mr. Udolpho?" he said, blinking stupidly.

"Yeh, yeh. You think it was Mr. Herbert Hoover?" The voice gargled in heavy Sicilian mirth over the simple jest. "Look, Usher: okay."

"Okay . . . ?"

"Yeh. Whatsa matter? You don't hear so good today?"

"Yes," Christopher said slowly. "I heard you; that is, I'm sure I did. You said okay?" It was unbelievable; he could not focus his thoughts properly. . . .

"Okay, okay." The voice sounded faintly impatient. "How many times you got to hear it. The dough: you get it."

"I see." Like an invalid recovering from shock, he felt the inertia of astonishment, the odd impossibility of adequate reaction. "You mean," he said, "that you've agreed to pay the increase?"

"I tell you what," said Udolpho, "I feel generous. So okay: I'm gonna give you the dough. This time," he said, a note of warning invading the soft voice. "That don't mean you can try it again. But this time, okay. You got it." Again the faraway chuckle sounded. "Whatsa matter?" he said. "You surprised? You ain't saying nothing. You didn't think you'd get it, hey?"

"No, no, it's not that." He spoke with the most extreme

difficulty; inside him, strange things seemed to be happening. "That is to say, naturally I hoped you'd see it my way. Of course when you didn't call yesterday, I wondered—"

"I was too busy," he said, brushing aside, in the brief phrase, twenty-four hours of indecision and heartbreak. "But you know now okay. You want me to tell Flair?"

"No," said Christopher quickly; slowly, the picture had begun to take shape. "No, I'd prefer to tell him, if you don't mind. I'd much prefer to tell him." There was, he realized, the necessity for expressed gratitude. "I want to thank you, Mr. Udolpho. I assure you that you won't have any cause to regret this. . . ."

"I better not." It was a trifle grim; Christopher paid no attention; he did not even hear. "You got anything else on your mind?"

"No. Not a thing. Not a single thing. Only, of course, to thank you once again, and to say that you'll have no cause to regret—"

"Yeh, yeh," said Mr. Udolpho. "Good-by." For the day was still long in Chicago and he was a man with much to do; it was not in the prolongation of the inessential that business prospered and salves were sold. . . .

"Good-by," said Christopher softly, speaking to the already dead connection; absorbed in thought, he did not hang up until the voice of the operator sounded querulously in his ear.

He rose from his chair and stood very still, holding onto

the desk as if for support. For a moment his eyes seemed to mist, then clear. He let out his breath in a great, gasping exhalation; with one hand he stroked his side, over and over again, as if reassuring himself of the fact of his corporeal presence. He felt as if he were about to burst. . . .

Inside his head, lights glowed, rose and gold. Images shot by, across the surface of his brain, in brilliant and bewildering succession; from somewhere deep within his being came great, powerful surges of joy which threatened to lift him bodily from the floor. He wanted to yell. . . .

He felt like this for what seemed a long time; then the blinding euphoria diminished, and reason, sweet reason, took over. In a relative calm, Christopher began the assessment of his position. He stood alone in one small, quiet room; through the walls came the muted clatter of the teletype machine, spelling out its message of victory and defeat, growth and decay—the snatches of the human adventure, from every corner of the world. Christopher heard it and smiled gently; at this moment, it had become something symbolic. . . .

It had been a bad night, a bad day. He had gone down to depths he had never before known; he had experienced bitterness, betrayal, despair, darkness of soul. Yet somehow, as always for him, the forces of justice had prevailed. He had gone down deep, but he had come up strong; now as before, there was a glorious equity between performance and reward. Before him—before him loomed new heights. Adversity had left him scarred, but the scar

215

tissue was stronger than before. He had been strengthened: from the purgatory of his experience he had emerged sharper, purer, wiser, ready for the task ahead.

He paused to balance, now, what he had lost, what he had gained. He knew, with a faint and transient twinge, that he would miss and he would mourn; yet even in this sober instant of consideration, the new excitement carried him on. For the truth—the one, magnificent inescapable truth—was that in the largest sense he had *not* lost: that, spread far-flung across a continent, a great, extended, loyal brotherhood still waited—and now he knew they would not wait in vain. The world, he knew, seemed at times a grim place; to find the sunshine that blossomed from the human heart, to spread the fact of that sunshine to others, was not an easy task in a world gone mad. Yet it was *his* task, and at the thought of five million hopeful people— now, soon, possibly more—listening to him night after night, far into the glorious tomorrow, his eyes became moist, and he vowed that he would not fail.

The evening of the fine fall day approached rapidly; outside, it was getting dark. Christopher moved from behind his desk and stepped smartly toward the door. Before the day ended there was work to be done; before the day ended, he had one thing to which he must certainly attend.

And so, serene in heart, peaceful in mind, and steady of purpose, he went off whistling to bring the good news to Adam Flair. . . .